FRANCES ELLEN

A Queen To Come

Contents

Chapter 1

It was a cold October morning on the magically protected and undetectable island of Saluverus. Nineteen-year-old Affinite Jacob Henderson shoved his hands into his pockets as he made his way down the
steps of the massive castle and towards the arena. Jacob wasn't the only
one heading there; thousands of other Affinites were streaming in from
the other direction; from the town at the bottom of the cliffs and up the
thousand steps towards the arena.

All to get a good seat for the Asters' open training that was starting in
half an hour's time.

It wasn't every day that Affinites were allowed to come and watch
the five Asters train. They were the five most powerful creatures in
the world; each possessing a magic that was completely unique. They
usually trained in private.

But not today.

Jacob strode along the walkway that connected the castle to the arena.
Both were built up against, and half into, the cliffs along the long
western side of the island. Those cliffs towered over the rest of the
island, leaving the town down below in shadows for the better part of
each afternoon, when the sun would disappear behind the tall rock face.

Jacob hunched his shoulders against the chill. His sandy blonde hair
blew around his face in the wind. He buried his hands deeper into the
pockets of his leather jacket. The jacket was too thin to really keep him

warm, but the walk from the castle was so short that Jacob didn't mind suffering the cold for a few minutes.

The island lay in the Norwegian Sea, between Iceland and Norway. Around this time of year the skies were a pale blue most of the time, without a cloud to be seen, but it was always cold. Jacob didn't mind it. Despite the temperature, the island always had a warm and homely feeling about it. On either side of the walkway the ground was covered in sea asters. Usually those star-like flowers only grew on the sea shores, as their name would suggest, and bloomed from mid-summer through to September, but still now the grass was covered in the little white and purple flowers. It was the magic in them. Only on this island, created especially by a woman so powerful, did these special flowers bloom all year long and on every available strip of grass.

Darren, a close friend of Jacob's, was waiting for him at the entrance to the arena. The enormous stadium was a similar size to the Colosseum in Rome. Jacob himself trained there every other day, though he would never in a million years get an audience like this one.

Jacob and Darren followed the crowds into the arena and wound up sitting at the top of the first tier of the stands, which gave them a clear view of the arena floor below. No one was on the floor yet; there wouldn't be for another fifteen minutes, but the stands were almost completely filled already. There hadn't been an open training for months, and most of the Affinites in town had jumped at the opportunity to watch the legendary Asters as their trainer tested them and pushed their magical abilities to their limits.

Jacob used to dream of being an Aster; it was possible to become one without having inherited it from a parent. He dreamed about it sometimes still. But for now he would have to make do with being just an Affinite. Jacob had a unique affinity, just like every other Affinite in these stands. It was what set them all apart from the millions of humans that lived on the continents of the earth. Humans didn't know of Affinite and Aster existence, and never would. If they ever witnessed either an Affinite or Aster in action their memories would be selectively wiped. But it was up to Asters and Affinites to protect the humans of the world from Dark Magic. Or more specifically, it was up to the five Asters. Only if a war broke out would Affinites be called into battle, though that hadn't happened for twenty-five years.

"So, who came first, the Affinites or the Asters?"

Jacob turned his head at the familiar voice of his former primary school teacher, Mrs. Emsworth. She was walking along the row of seats one level beneath where Jacob and Darren were sitting. Behind her trailed fifteen eight-year-olds all eager and staring wide-eyed all around the arena.

"Affinites!" called one girl from the back.

Mrs. Emsworth looked up and caught Jacob's eye and smiled, recognizing him. "That's right. They lived among humans for centuries in peace, didn't they? And when did that peace change?"

In the dark ages, Jacob thought to himself.

"At the beginning of the Dark Ages," a boy right behind Mrs. Emsworth whispered.

Mrs. Emsworth sat down on the bench beneath Jacob and Darren, and gestured for the children to follow suit. "You are right, Tommy," Mrs. Emsworth said. "So, at the beginning of the Dark Ages, about one thousand years ago, there was a celestial event that changed everything. What event was that?"

"The Blood Solstice!" a dark-skinned boy cried.

Jacob smirked at the boy's enthusiasm and turned his attention back to the floor of the arena. Mrs. Emsworth continued to quiz her students on the history of Affinites and Asters. Every Affinite in the world knew the story she was about to tell them. It was the story of their people. Of how so much dark energy came with the Blood Solstice – when there was a blood moon on the same night as a winter solstice – that seven

Affinite brothers decided to take the power for themselves and became immortal in the process. Their souls corrupted as they did so, giving in to the forces of greed, lust and anger. They called themselves the seven Higher Kings, and they took over the world with their Dark Magic. The Kings spread out, taking over one continent each. Affinites drawn to the allure of their Dark Magic had their souls corrupted just like the Kings, and became Dark Disciples. They still had control over their affinity, but they served a King.

Mrs. Emsworth left no part out as she told her students the story. She explained how humans were taken as slaves and how Affinites were hunted for sport. There was no light, only darkness and destruction. Affinites had to go into hiding, living deep in the mountains and forests to remain undetected. Scattered across the world the Affinites stood no chance against the Kings' mighty rule.

"Look at them staring," Darren whispered in Jacob's ear. Jacob looked down. Darren was right: every one of the students was gaping at their teacher with their eyes wide. Jacob doubted any of these children didn't already know every little detail of their bloody history. The story was part of who they were; how they were brought up. Just like how every young Affinite was trained to enhance their natural resilience to the violence and fighting they could possibly experience. The fact that these eight-year-olds were here to watch a training where the Asters would be pushed to their limits and near death, with only healing magic to save them, was precisely for that reason.

Mrs. Emsworth looked at each of the children and said in a heavy voice, "For five hundred years the Kings ruled the world. For five hundred years they destroyed everything that was good and pure. But it wasn't enough for them. When the Blood Solstice came around again, they wanted more. But there was one young girl who wanted it all to end. Her name was Aiyana."

Jacob hated himself for feeling a flutter at the bottom of his stomach.

He was a man; he was nineteen-years-old, and yet he still felt that same flicker of excitement every time someone talked about Aiyana. She was... something else. She had lost her father to a Disciple; she wasn't a fighter and couldn't save him when her village on the shores of Denmark was attacked. There had been a ship waiting on the coast, ready to take any Affinite still alive to find a land that was safe. Aiyana boarded that ship and brought along her favourite flowers that grew along the Danish shore: sea asters.

The story went that Aiyana held those flowers as she prayed to the stars. She prayed for someone to hear her, to one day put an end to the Darkness and make a place of true safety so that she could bring light back to the world again.

But the ship capsized in a storm. And Aiyana drowned.

But the stars answered. Legend said that the sky filled with brightness, and lightning shot out of the sky and hit Aiyana where she drifted lifelessly in the water. And from the depths underneath her the ground started to rise, and it brought her up to the surface. And she was born again, not as human, but as something greater. She possessed a magic so strong that she expanded the land that had raised her up. She made it larger, had one side be a towering cliff face, and covered the entire northern quarter with a thick forest of pine trees. She covered most of the rest of the flat, grassy land with her favourite flowers and she cast a spell to make sure no Darkness could ever see it. And she called it Saluverus.

She used her magic to bring the few thousand surviving Affinites in the world to this one island. From each corner of the world, of all religions and cultures, the Affinites came together. On Saluverus they were safe. Once settled, they had started training to form an army capable of challenging the Kings.

Aiyana's magic was colossal: she could talk to animals and turn into them, and use their strengths. She was also super-humanly strong and fast. She could heal the wounded with the touch of her hand. She could stop herself from feeling pain if she got an injury so she could keep fighting or find shelter so she could recover, and she could heal herself if the injuries were too severe. And she could control the earth's nature around her. She could create holes in the ground that swallowed up her enemies. She could command trees and vines and roots to move to trap her opponents.

But she knew she couldn't win the war by herself. Her magic was too concentrated. It was incredible magic, but it would need to be spread out over the lines of her army to be the most effective. So, she went to a field of sea asters she had grown herself, and cast one great spell. She split her magic, creating six separate ones: Health and Knowledge, Speed and Flight, Strength, Flora, Endurance, and Analgesia. The magic of Fauna, of animals, she kept herself. She gave each magic to an Affinite originally from a different continent. And finally, she called them the Asters, after her favourite flower that reminded her of home, to which she would never return.

It was the descendants of those original six Asters that Jacob, Darren, and the rest of Saluverus had come here to see today. The magic of the Asters had lived on through generations. The exception was Aiyana's; the magic of Fauna had died with her.

Until eighteen years ago.

"Because, what happened eighteen years ago?" Mrs. Emsworth asked her students.

All the children shouted their answers at the same time.

"The Queen was born!"

"Aiyana came back!"

"Her magic was born again!"

Mrs. Emsworth laughed and held up her hand to try and calm the children down. "That's right. After almost five hundred years a girl was born with Queen Aiyana's magic of Fauna. And do we know the name of that girl?"

"Gayle Mendosa! Gayle Mendosa!" the kids all screamed.

Jacob chuckled at the sight of Mrs. Emsworth trying to shush the children, but she couldn't stop them from shouting loudly at each other that the Queen had finally returned, that her magic was born again, and that, after eighteen years of being brought up away from Saluverus, Gayle Mendosa, Queen Aiyana's reincarnation, was coming home.

There was another flutter in the pit of Jacob's stomach at that thought. The Queen was coming home. The most powerful creature to ever walk on this earth had been reborn in his lifetime. From the moment he had heard this, he had trained harder than ever before. He wanted to be the best soldier on Saluverus, so that when a war would come, his only place would be by the Queen's side.

Because war would come. For all the excitement and anticipation and celebration when Gayle Mendosa was born with Queen Aiyana's magic, there was also dread and fear. Aiyana's magic was only created when there was a dire need of it: to bring balance back into the world. Gayle Mendosa would not have been born with the same magic if that balance was secure. Her magical birth predicted a threat to the peaceful existence that the past five hundred years of Aster generations had created and protected.

The double doors to the arena floor opened and silence fell. Even the children in the row below Jacob stopped making a noise and turned their attention to see who had arrived.

Sky Mayne, the Aster of Speed and Flight, stepped onto the grounds, a short, black spear gleaming in his hands. Unlike regular trainings, where everyone wore whatever they found most comfortable, Sky was now wearing traditional training gear, which consisted of black trousers that were looser around the thighs and calves, but tight with an elastic band around the ankles, and a simple black, stretch top. Jacob clenched his fists by his side as he watched Sky swagger to the centre of the arena.

The crowd resumed its eager chatter. Behind Jacob, a group of girls were giggling and whispering excitedly. Sensing the attention, Sky looked up at the stand, pushing his golden blonde hair out of his face and flashing a dazzling grin. His gaze passed over Jacob, hardening slightly in recognition, before moving on. Then his lips curved into a devilish smile and his dark blue eyes sparkled as he winked at the group of girls sitting behind Jacob and Darren. The girls giggled even louder, and one of them practically shrieked at the attention Sky was giving them.

Jacob rolled his eyes at the sheer arrogance of the Aster. "God, he's so full of himself," he muttered.

"Is it all for show or is he genuinely like that?" Darren asked.

Jacob watched how Sky leaned nonchalantly on his spear as he let his charming smile reach more giddy girls. "He's genuinely like that."

And Jacob would know. He actually trained with the Aster of Speed. Jacob's affinity was that of strategy. Every Affinite that had an affinity that could be advantageous in battle followed additional combat train-ing. And the best Affinites were brought to Saluverus and trained with the five Asters several times a week.

And Jacob was one of the best. He had to be, for what he wanted: to fight alongside the new Queen.

During those sessions the Asters weren't allowed to use their magic, so it was an even playing field. Jacob had trained with Sky before, and he could truthfully say that none of this showy, cocky, charming behaviour was an act. Sky was known for being the *greatest Aster of his generation*, and boy, he never let anyone forget it. Especially Jacob. And so Jacob had made it his personal goal to annoy and belittle Sky whenever he could, just to take him down a peg or two.

The arena doors opened again and Matu Madaki stepped inside. Originally from Nairobi, Kenya, the Aster of Strength had the physique of a professional American footballer. He was at least six and a half feet tall, with his arms, shoulders and chest packed with muscle. He had dark skin, even darker eyes and a shaven head.

Matu Madaki was the complete opposite to Sky. Where Sky was rash and daring, Matu was rational and strategic. He was the calm-in-a-storm type; always thinking, always planning. Whatever the best way out of a bad situation would be, Matu would think of it. Sky would impulsively do the first thing that came to mind without thinking about the longer-term consequences.

Matu walked over to Sky and said something no one in the stands could hear over the constant talking and laughing of the crowd. As the two Asters talked, Matu grazed his fingers over the knuckle knives he wore. It was a contraption with four holes for Matu to stick his fingers through, but on the thumb-side of the hole for his index finger, a small blade gleamed in the artificial lighting of the arena. Those things were truly deadly. Matu's magic of Strength made him dangerous enough; he could break half the bones in your face with a single punch, but with the flick of his wrist, he could simultaneously slice your throat with that blade.

Matu always carried a sword with him as well, though Jacob had never actually seen the Aster use it. Thanks to his magic, his hands were usually deadly enough.

The Aster of Strength said something that made Sky laugh. A girly gasp came from behind Jacob together with the words, "Did you hear that? Oh, I love the way he laughs!"

Jacob gave his friend a look before turning his head to see which of the girls had said such an embarrassing thing. To his surprise, Jacob recognised the girl from his history class. Her name was Grace and she was staring down at the two Asters with desperate infatuation.

Jacob looked back at Darren who was trying to keep himself from laughing. Jacob sniggered and looked at his watch. Five more minutes before the open training was to start.

The doors opened again, and this time two Asters stepped inside. Jacob had less of an aversion to these two. On the left was San Francisco-born Nathan Radbourne, the Aster of Flora. He had brown hair and brown eyes. He was tall and muscular, but didn't have the big shoulders, arms and chest that Matu had. Two broadswords were strapped across his back in an X. Nathan was quite a mystery. The boy seemed to have two personalities; on the training grounds he was cold, clinical and fierce, while outside of training he was extremely quiet, on the edge of unsure and insecure.

"Now *he's* cute," one of Grace's friends breathed as Nathan walked over to the centre of the arena.

"No, I like Matu better," another girl said.

"I hear he's taken," Grace said. "Sky on the other hand..."

Will sleep with you once and never call you again, Jacob thought to himself. Sky Mayne had that reputation, and it was astounding that these girls didn't know about it. Or maybe they did and they just didn't care. Sky was an Aster after all, a prize in itself to some girls.

Jacob grunted at the thought, though when his gaze settled on the girl walking beside Nathan Radbourne, his frustrations about Sky seemed to disappear.

Sophie Griffiths, the Aster of Health and Knowledge, was originally from London, the same as Jacob. She didn't have a particularly pretty face, but her thunderstorm grey eyes were something to behold. She had her long blonde hair tied in a single plait down her back. Her signature miniature crossbow was tied to her left wrist, and her deadly rapier sword was in its sheath at her right side. Jacob tried not to stare as Sophie walked up to the three male Asters. Though they were all taller and much more muscular than her, she was definitely not cowed by them. On the contrary; she radiated a quiet self-confidence, and Jacob knew that she had all the Aster boys wrapped around her finger.

"Now there's a bad-ass woman," one of Grace's friends breathed in awe. Finally, something the girls said that Jacob could agree with. He looked over his shoulder to the straight haired, mousy-faced girl on Grace's right.

Grace put an arm around the girl. "I'm sorry to have to tell you, my friend, but I don't think she's into girls."

From the corner of his eye, Jacob saw the girl look at Sophie for a moment longer. "How are you so sure?"

Grace snorted. "Trust me on that one. Remember Manuela? The Spanish girl from our second year? She tried. And she didn't fail because she was unattractive, because... well, you've seen her."

"She came on to Sophie? Seriously?" the girl asked.

"Tried and failed, my friend. She was convinced Sophie was like her. Trust me, she's not. Plus, she dated Arthur Kelly for a few months last year."

Jacob turned his attention away from the girl-talk behind him, for the doors opened one last time. Two figures stepped through. The first was Lian Fai, the last of the Asters. Originally from Tokyo, Lian had short, spiky, black hair and dark brown eyes. He was the Aster of Analgesia. In other words: he could feel no pain. He would die as soon as anyone else, but no matter how extensive the injury, it wouldn't hurt him. He could keep fighting until his body physically couldn't anymore. It made him deadly and unpredictable, because he could surprisingly keep coming at you while sporting an injury that would've stopped other opponents right in their tracks.

A hush fell over the crowd when everyone recognised the second figure walking onto the grounds. It was Jackson Kelly, the Commanding Chief, and the personal trainer of the Asters. He was also in charge of all the combat trainings for the Affinites, but he rarely ever gave those himself. The Asters were his main priority, for they were the first line of defence if any of the Kings would ever come crawling out from the Underworld, where Aiyana and her army had banished them, and make a play for the

Surface of the earth.

The five Asters stood in a straight line and faced the Commanding Chief. The arena was so quiet you could hear a pin drop. Jacob glanced at his watch. Nine o'clock. Bang on time.

The training was about to begin.

Chapter 2

A few minutes earlier Sky Mayne was the only one on the grounds of the arena. The stands were filling rapidly as he entered. He held his hand up and waved to the crowd. He caught the eye of a group of girls near the top of the first tier of stands across from him and winked at them. Jacob bloody Henderson was sitting just beneath them, he noticed, sourly. Quite deliberately, to rile him, Sky grinned wickedly at one of the girls, who literally shrieked in Jacob's ear.

Jacob was the reason Sky had mixed feelings about the trainings the Asters shared with the best Affinites of their age. Sky had made a few great Affinite friends through those trainings, but Jacob was an absolute nightmare. Sky knew the boy was jealous, and wanted desperately to be an Aster. That didn't mean Jacob had to push all the wrong buttons on purpose. Sky had made a point, long ago, to push all the wrong buttons back in return. And so a searing hatred had been born. Sky shook himself and turned his attention away from Jacob.

Sky always loved these open trainings, where Affinites were allowed to come in and watch as they practised. He enjoyed the cheering, and the *oohs* and *aahs* as he flew by. For him that was the best part of his magic of Speed and Flight: flying. Sure, the being able to run super-humanly fast bit had its perks. And he could shimmer to any place in the world in the blink of an eye, which wasn't so bad either. But the flying... he never felt as free as he did when he was soaring over the tree tops of the old pine forest at the north corner of Saluverus, or when he would let himself drop from the cliffs and only start flying a millisecond before he hit the waters of the Norwegian Sea below.

His magic made him strong—powerful even. *The greatest Aster of his generation.* That's what Sky Mayne was. That's what they called him, and he revelled in it. He made sure no one forgot it.

As he made his way to the centre of the arena, in his black training gear and with his signature short spear resting nonchalantly across his shoulders, he could already hear the whispering. Yes, the blonde one. Yes, the one with the dark blue eyes. Yes, yes, yes, that was the greatest of them all.

Sky flashed his grin to all the admiring eyes looking down on him. He pushed back his blonde hair and winked at another girl near the top. Even from this distance he saw her blush and smile, star-struck, back at him.

"Are you done?"

Sky turned around, grinning, to his brother, Matu Madaki, the Aster of Strength. He wasn't a brother by blood, but a brother by magic. Where Matu's family originated from Kenya, Sky's came from Australia.

"Never, mate" Sky said. For all the years he had lived on Saluverus he had made sure that he never lost his Australian accent. Every Affinite who lived here who wasn't originally from an English-speaking country grew up speaking with an American accent. So, Sky made sure he stayed his unique self. The ladies never failed to love him all the more for it.

Matu shook his head, a hint of a smile on his face. He wiggled his fingers in his signature knuckle knives. He had a single sword strapped to his belt, but Sky doubted Matu would even touch it. Being the Aster of Strength, Matu's greatest weapons were his hands. Any blade would just get in the way. If he got a good punch in, he was just as effective, maybe even more so, than if he'd use any kind of weapon.

Sky leaned on his spear. "It's not my fault they throw themselves at me."

Matu gave Sky a look over his shoulder. "I'm not having this conversation again."

"They'd throw themselves at you, too, if you'd let them," Sky pushed.

Matu rolled his eyes and looked back past Sky to the doors that led into the grounds. "*Taken.*"

"Josie's in Canada! You're worthy of so much more than some long-distance thing," Sky exclaimed.

Matu cocked his head to the left. "Are you done?"

Sky shrugged and turned around to where Matu was looking. "Your loss."

The crowd's talking grew even louder as the doors to the grounds opened again and Sophie and Nathan stepped through. Nathan had his usual broadswords strapped to his back, while Sophie was wearing her signature miniature crossbow on her left wrist. In the sheath at her right side was a rapier sword.

Sophie's long blonde hair was tied in a single plait down her back, and her thunderstorm grey eyes were alert and focused. She paid no attention to the crowd as she strode to the centre of the arena with her head held high. Right now, it was hard to believe she could be perceived as bubbly and witty; she looked so cold and brutal, with her set expression, and in her black training gear. Same as Matu, Sophie and Nathan were like siblings to Sky. He was fiercely protective of Sophie, even though she was more than capable of holding her own against anyone dumb enough to try and hurt her. Sky loved joking around with his siblings, though he picked on Nathan more, because he was two years younger at eighteen, than he would of Matu, who was older.

Sophie and Nathan came to stand beside Sky and Matu, and waited for the final Aster and their trainer to enter the arena.

"It's filling up," Sophie observed as she scanned the stands, her English accent coming through clearly. She was right. The stands were almost completely full now, with Affinites of all ages. The Asters rarely did open trainings anymore and everyone had jumped at the opportunity to see *the legendary Asters* train for whenever Affinites and humans would need their protection. More than half of the town had come to watch. They could almost feel the excitement and anticipation radiate off of the crowd.

Sky took it all in. "I miss this."

"We're not here for them," Nathan pointed out.

Sky turned to look at his brother who was usually so warm and quiet. The deadly cold had descended upon him now as he clenched his fists by his side, readying himself for the training. "Don't take all the fun out of it."

"We're not circus animals," Nathan muttered.

"Don't be so dramatic," Sky breathed.

"Oh, he's not," Sophie interjected. "In open trainings you're dramatic enough for all of us." She turned her head to Sky and grinned.

Sky eyed his sister narrowly. "I call it theatrical."

On his other side, Nathan shook his head, but before he or Sophie could say anything else Lian Fai, the Aster of Analgesia, stepped into the arena. He had his bow and quiver slung across his shoulder. A sword hung at his side and two daggers were sheathed to his forearms.

Originally from Tokyo, Japan, Lian was the most skilled fighter of them all. He had to be; his magic caused him not to feel any of the pain that was inflicted upon him. It made him extremely dangerous since, even with life-threatening wounds, he would be able to keep fighting when an opponent wouldn't expect him to be able to.

Lian raked a hand through his short, spiky, black hair and glanced up at the stands. There was more pointing and whispering, until it all suddenly stopped. Behind Lian, the doors never fully closed before another figure appeared.

Jackson Kelly, the Commanding Chief and the Asters' trainer, stepped into the grounds.

Originally from Iceland, Jackson and his brother Percy were the strongest Affinite soldiers in the war fought by the Asters' parents twenty-five years earlier. They both had the affinity for bravery and, after the war, had been asked to lead the training programmes for the Asters and Affinites alike.

The gigantic, broad-shouldered ex-soldier strode into the silent arena. Jackson stopped in front of the Asters, who each inclined their heads in respect. Jackson nodded to the Asters before turning his attention to the stands.

"Welcome," he bellowed, "to an Asters Open Training. You will watch as I test them for thirty minutes, three times. Don't worry. A magical barrier will protect you from any weapons that might come your way. And now, without further ado—" Jackson turned to the Asters and said, "—let's begin."

Thirty seconds.

They had thirty seconds from the moment Jackson stepped away from them until the first of the attacks would begin.

Jackson vanished into the control room, where he would sit at the control panels behind one-way glass, so he could see what the Asters were doing but the Asters couldn't see him.

Even so, Sophie knew the first button he would push. A sizzling sound was her confirmation. The magical barrier that protected the onlookers from any danger was going up. When no one came to watch the barrier was never raised and the stands would be used as part of the training. The roof to the arena was closed today, but Jackson would have the roof open a lot during other trainings, too. He would take advantage of whatever Scandinavian weather was raging outside to prepare the Asters for anything they might encounter on missions.

Ten more seconds and the training would start.

In the first thirty-minute session all the Asters were on the same side. They were to keep themselves and each other alive and unharmed for the whole thirty minutes, while also keeping a single, small, red ball from ever touching the ground. For the second thirty minutes they would be divided into a team of two and a team of three, where they would not only have to avoid whatever Jackson threw at them, but they would also have to beat the other team. To beat the other team was to genuinely fight until death, without actually delivering the killing blow. In the final thirty minutes it was every man for himself. Or *woman*, in Sophie's case. In that final session it was an Aster's goal to be the last one standing.

Five more seconds.

Sophie scanned the grounds. All along the arena walls were a variety of different-sized ledges that the Asters could make use of. A wide range of monkey bars and concrete blocks were distributed around the grounds as well. The Asters had positioned themselves along the walls of the arena equidistant from one another. That was where Jackson always ordered them to start. Where they moved next was up to them.

Sophie flexed her left hand. She grazed her thumb over the small button on the side of her index finger that would release a small but deadly bolt from the miniature crossbow around her left wrist. She put her left foot slightly behind her right and waited.

There was no bell that told them the training had started. The first Sophie knew of it was the knife that shot from the other wall straight at her heart. She spun to the side, the knife embedding itself deep into the wall behind her.

And then the action was everywhere. Weapons fired at them from every direction, obstacles burst up out of the ground, trying to off-balance the Asters enough for one of them to drop the red ball or miss throwing it to someone else. Sophie knew Sky had started with the small red ball, but while she'd spun away from the knife, she heard Matu call "Got it!" to her left.

There was magic in the floor and in every other inch of the arena. Jackson didn't possess magic of his own, but he could command the magic in the arena with the control panels. Through the magic he could also command a set of mannequins that could move as if alive. They were exactly like mannequins you would find in a clothes store. Except these weren't actually wearing clothes and they were made of stronger material. They didn't have hair or any other defining features, not even a mouth or a nose or eyes. Their heads were like eggs: smooth and oval-shaped. They were spelled to have Disciple instincts and they could wield weapons. They couldn't move as quickly or with as much fluidity as a Disciple, but they were real enough, and they were spelled so they'd only go down if the attack would take down a Disciple in real life.

Sophie climbed up to a high ledge close to where the stands started, by using hand and footholds similar to those used for indoor rock climbing. From her perch she watched as Matu barely broke sweat as he brought a mannequin to its knees with one swift punch across its face. Sophie had fought alongside Matu long enough to expect the sound of bones crunching each time he came into contact with an attacker. She had got used to it by now. The same way as she was used to Lian barely ever avoiding blows in one-to-one combat. The surprise of him not darting away to miss the attack often gave Lian the opening he needed to make the kill. Though this left him open to injuries that he sometimes didn't even realise were life-threatening. If it wasn't for Sophie, Lian would've been dead ten times over already. Lian's blind loyalty and honour led him to often take the brunt of an attack when the Asters were sent out on missions. It was incredibly brave, but could also be fatal if Sophie wasn't close enough to save him.

And he knew it. Sophie's magic of Health and Knowledge was why each of the boys could go to their absolute limit. She could heal them when they were on the brink of death. Sophie never thought about how many times one of her brothers would've died if she hadn't been there in time. Each one of those times was a time too many. She herself had to be more careful because she was unable to use her magic to heal herself. For that, one of her brothers needed to use her blood to harness her magic for that purpose.

But it was Lian who Sophie stayed closest to. He was the only one of them who didn't seem to know the concept of self-preservation. It made him incredibly dangerous to their enemies, but a martyr if Sophie wasn't close enough.

Now again, Lian was fighting a mannequin while a knife was flying towards the both of them. The mannequin ducked because of the magic controlling it, but Lian didn't. The knife buried itself in his abdomen, but Lian barely flinched as he brought his sword down.

"Sophie!"

Sophie tore her eyes away from Lian long enough to spot the red ball flying towards her. Nathan had thrown it from where he was balancing on the top of a tall set of monkey bars in the centre of the arena. Sophie caught it with her free right hand; her rapier was still in its sheath at her hip.

She turned her attention back to Lian. The surprise of not ducking away from the knife had given him the time to take down the mannequin. When he was about to step away from his kill, however, he was swaying and looking down at the knife in his abdomen. Sophie knew she had to get there fast.

From where she was squatting she could see how another two mannequins were already heading towards Lian, and she knew that he would keep fighting until his body physically couldn't anymore.

Sophie aimed her wrist crossbow at one of the mannequins heading Lian's way and pressed the button with her thumb. The small bolt hit the mannequin right in the eye and it collapsed to the ground. She then jumped down from her perch onto a lower block of concrete, still about five feet above the ground. As she landed, she could see Lian's blood was starting to coat the floor as he pushed the other mannequin back.

Sophie was about to jump to the ground when a mannequin rose up right at her feet, a sword in its hand. But before she could quickly unsheathe her rapier there was a blue flash, and Sky had used his shimmer to appear right above her. He crashed down on top of the mannequin, his short spear held tight in both hands, to give Sophie a clear route towards Lian.

There was an *oooh* from the crowd as Sky brought the mannequin crashing down, but Sophie paid no attention. She knew Sky would be smiling. Somehow, he always found time to smile in trainings like these. She would be, too, if she could just vanish and re-appear wherever she wanted, at will.

Sophie jumped down and ran towards where Lian was fighting with a strength no man should be able to with the wound he had. He stumbled a step back but still managed to block a blow from the mannequin with his sword, while also avoiding an arrow that was heading right in his direction.

It made Sophie scowl. Jackson wasn't taking it easy on them.

Her breathing ragged, Sophie called out Lian's name to let him know she was coming to him. She knew her call was what Lian had been waiting for. With three swift motions that completely dislodged the knife in his abdomen, letting the blood run free, which would kill him in minutes, Lian cut down the mannequin in front of him. But before he could turn to Sophie to get himself healed, he saw the exact same thing

Sophie did that made her stop in her tracks as well.

Across the arena, Matu was breaking down several brick walls that Jackson had made shoot out of the ground and block his path. Without knowing that a mannequin was waiting on the other side, ready to bring down its sword, Matu threw his magic into his fists and punched through the final wall.

The mannequin rose up in front of Matu, and before he could do anything to stop the sword from coming down, the mannequin was thrown to the side, simultaneously impaled through the chest by the sword Lian had thrown, and pierced through the neck by a small bolt Sophie had let loose from her wrist crossbow.

Neither Sophie nor Lian gave Matu a second look. Sophie knew Lian couldn't have thrown that sword if she hadn't been on her way already. That throw alone had turned his survival rate with an abdomen wound like his from minutes to seconds. And even though he couldn't feel the pain, Lian would be able to sense how close the injury was to killing him.

Lian stumbled back again, but Sophie was there. Before she could lay her right hand on him and let her magic work, she needed to get rid of the ball.

"Sky!" Sophie yelled. She tightened her fingers around the small red ball and threw it up into the air.

She had no idea where Sky had been at the time she called his name. But she knew he was there because she caught the blue flash of Sky's magical shimmer from the corner of her eye. The gasps and cheers from the crowd told her he had caught it, and the game was still on. She quickly laid her right hand on Lian's abdomen and let her magic work. The black Band around her wrist, that looked like a tattooed bracelet, glowed golden, indicating her magic was active. In less than ten seconds there was nothing left of Lian's wound except for the torn shirt and some dried blood.

Lian didn't bother to thank her; they never thanked each other for the use of their magic. There was never any time. Within seconds Lian was back on his feet and swerving to the side to avoid yet another two knives thrown his way.

Sophie didn't have time to watch him go as the floor underneath her feet groaned and started to crumble away. A second later she was rolling and throwing herself towards solid ground, while also avoiding the mannequins and the weapons that Jackson was so accurately directing at her.

And all the while the crowd kept cheering, watching with wide eyes and open mouths, and clapping whenever one of the Asters pulled off an incredible move or unexpectedly managed to save another. But Sophie didn't hear them. There was just the lethal calm of the simulated battle as the seconds and minutes ticked away.

Chapter 3

The chatter and laughter of the crowd as they started filing out of the arena could be heard from the closed rooms beneath the stands. After waving at the crowd and taking a deep bow at the end of their training the five Asters headed for the weapons room. This small rectangular space was in the part of the arena that was built into the cliffs and had no windows to let in daylight. Bright, artificial lighting turned on automatically the second Sky opened the door; the rest of the Asters walked in behind him.

Sky headed for the large round table in the centre of the room and dropped his short spear onto it. At the same time Sophie began the task of healing whatever injuries the Asters still had. In the third round of the training a whip had magically coiled its way around Matu's ankle and had pulled his feet out from underneath him. He had broken his wrist as he landed, and now he was groaning slightly as Sophie's healing magic worked its way through his bones. Sky could almost hear them snap back together, and he watched as Sophie stepped back and Matu wriggled his fingers painlessly.

"That could've gone better," Matu muttered. He inclined his head to Sophie before coming up to Sky's side and sliding the knuckle knives off his hands. He dropped them on the table.

"You'd better not be talking about my healing," Sophie said. She had moved to the long wall, in front of which stood six large lockers, side by side. She opened the one that was hers and hung up her rapier and sheath on the back, and placed her wrist crossbow on the bottom.

Matu looked over his shoulder. "You know I'm not."

"At least you didn't fall on your face," Lian joked. "Though I'd pay good money to see that."

"Shut up," Matu said, tugging off his jacket.

"Maybe Nate could grow a little patch of grass next time to soften your landing?" Sky offered.

Matu shot him a look, but Sky just grinned, winking at Lian who snickered behind him.

"Nate should have enough time to do that when all this is for real, you know. Even while battling Disciples right alongside you, he should be able to take a moment's break to help soften your fall. Hey Nate," Sky said, turning to his other brother, "maybe we can try it out next time we're out in the field?"

Nathan looked up. He remained quiet but the corners of his mouth twitched slightly as he held up his right hand. The black Band around his wrist started to glow green as Nathan put his magic to work.

Matu held up his hands. "No, *noo*. Stop it."

But it was already happening. Right underneath Matu's feet, the concrete gave way and, in its place, little sprouts of green grass shot up into the air.

Matu let out a sigh as he watched the grass grow thicker under his feet. "This is ridiculous."

Sophie and Lian looked on with quiet amusement, waiting to see how the exchange would play out.

Sky looked from the grass back to Nathan. "I think you're going to need it to be bigger. If you pull on his ankle right now his face will still hit concrete."

Nathan pretended to study his work with narrowed eyes. He then glanced at Sky. "You think?"

Sky grinned and nodded. "Definitely."

Nathan shrugged. The Band on his wrist started glowing again. The Band was in the shape of a thick bracelet, wrapping all the way around his wrist. It was like a tattoo, except that it had never been inked onto his skin. Nathan had been born with it. It had the width of about two inches and it was filled with swirling black lines.

Sky looked at his own Band. It was identical to Nathan's except for two things. Sky's Band glowed blue whenever he used his magic, while Nathan's glowed green. And on the inside of his wrist there were no black swirling lines but an open circle with one single image: for Sky that was the image of a wing, representing his magic of Speed and Flight. For Nathan it was the image of a horse chestnut leaf, representing his magic of Flora.

Sky chuckled as the patch of grass at Matu's feet expanded rapidly.

Matu's expression grew bored as he said, "Are you finished?"

"Almost," Nathan mused.

Sophie giggled by the lockers, and Sky cast her an amused glance.

"There," Nathan declared. The grass was now a perfect two-yard circle, with Matu standing at its centre. "What do you think?"

Matu rolled his eyes. "Perfect. Can you get rid of it now?"

Nathan looked at him, surprise in his eyes. "Don't you want me to test it first?"

Matu frowned. "Test it? How are you going to AHH—"

Before Matu could finish his question Nathan had thrown his hand forward. A green vine suddenly appeared in his hand and shot out towards Matu's ankle. Quick as a flash, Nathan pulled the vine back, which ripped Matu's legs from underneath him.

Matu landed on his back with a thud and a grunt.

Lian grinned hugely, and Sophie struggled to contain her laughter as she asked, "Are you all right?"

"I'm fine," Matu grumbled as he got back to his feet.

"Soft as a pillow?" Nathan asked.

Matu glared at his youngest brother. "I'm not answering that."

Nathan thought for a moment before turning his head away, saying softly, "I might have to make a few tweaks..."

Sky turned from Nathan to Matu. He could barely keep in his laughter. Matu looked at him with a warning in his eyes. He mouthed *don't*. Sky rolled his eyes and turned his attention back to unbuckling the weapons belt from around his waist.

Nathan was quite a mystery half the time. The second they stepped out of the arena he had gone back to his quiet self. With him saying he needed to make a few tweaks... Sky couldn't tell if his brother was joking or not. If he wasn't, and Nathan would actually use this patch of grass out in the field, it would be absolutely brilliant.

Someone cleared their throat, and each Aster, still chatting and laughing, turned to the door. They immediately fell silent when they saw who was standing in the doorway.

Their Commanding Chief, Jackson Kelly, surveyed each of them with his piercing stare. Sky caught the flash of green on Nathan's wrist and knew that the grass and the vine had vanished.

"Chief," Matu said.

Jackson didn't bother with pleasantries as he said, "Axel wants to see you in the Board Room. Now."

"We don't get to clean up first?" Sophie asked.

"No," was the Chief's only response.

Jackson was already half out the door again when Sky asked, "What's it about?"

The Chief turned around, his piercing gaze highly alert. "It's about Gayle Mendosa."

"She's coming here early. That must be what this is about," Sophie said excitedly as the five Asters, still in their torn training clothes and covered in dried sweat and blood, hurried out of the arena and up the steps to the castle. The cold October wind whipped at their faces but they were still filled with too much adrenaline to notice. White and purple sea asters bloomed all alongside the stone walkway that connected a side entrance of the arena directly to the side of the castle. Down to their right the hundreds of Affinites who had come to watch the training were still filing out of the front doors of the arena and down the steps back to the town below.

"She can't be. They set a specific date for a reason," Matu said. "She wouldn't come sooner unless she was in grave danger. And we wouldn't be here right now if she were."

"She's coming," Sophie breathed. "I know she is."

Sky looked sideways at his sister. Her thunderstorm grey eyes were brighter ever since Jackson had mentioned Gayle Mendosa. Sky's heart tightened for his sister. He knew what it meant to her to have Queen Aiyana's reincarnation on Saluverus with them. He just hoped Axel would bring the news she so desperately wanted to hear.

Gayle's existence was a miracle in itself. She was the daughter of Tomas and Cara Mendosa, two Asters of the previous generation. Sky's mother had been a part of that generation. Just like Sophie, Lian and Nathan's mothers, and Matu's father.

Two Asters hardly ever fell in love. Their bonds were so much like siblings that romantic feelings rarely ever developed. It had only happened once before: about a hundred years ago. When that female

Aster had been pregnant she was expecting twins. Normally each Aster only ever had one child. It was like some rule of nature. The child would be born with the magic of the parent, and because it would be the only child, its powers would be as strong as in the previous generation. The magic would never be diluted because of a split between siblings. But when, a hundred years ago, two Asters had fallen in love, the woman had given birth to twins. One child inherited the Aster magic of the father, and the other the magic of the mother. It was nature's way of keeping the Aster magic pure and strong.

When Cara Mendosa got pregnant, everyone had expected her to be carrying twins.

But she wasn't.

What she had been carrying was far more incredible. A miracle, in fact.

When Gayle Mendosa was born, she didn't have either her father or her mother's Aster magic. No. She was born with a magic that hadn't existed for almost five hundred years.

Gayle Mendosa had been born with the magic that had only been possessed by the first and last Queen of the Asters and Affinites: the magic of Fauna. She was the reincarnation of Queen Aiyana. The lone wolf who had brought all Affinites together and made them into her pack. The creator of the Underworld, the mother of all Asters, and the slayer of Kings.

Aiyana's reincarnation could only mean one thing: a magic was needed that was stronger than what the Asters together possessed. They would be facing something that their magic alone wouldn't be able to defeat. That was what Gayle Mendosa represented: a salvation from whatever threat was about to be unleashed across the world.

Affinites all over the world had celebrated her birth. And inevitably the Underworld got wind of it. And they had tried to take Gayle for themselves. To raise her in Darkness. The Asters and the Small Council of the time had their own ideas on how to keep Gayle safe; Saluverus seeming the best option, since no form of Darkness could detect the island and therefore would never find it.

But the Mendosas had other plans. They saw Saluverus as a prison. One Gayle wouldn't be allowed to set foot off of for her entire childhood. Only when she was strong enough to protect herself would she be allowed to step out into the world, if then.

No, the Mendosas wouldn't let their child live that way. So they left Saluverus. They decided to cloak themselves and Gayle, so their magic would be as undetectable as the island of Saluverus itself. And they would have a human life. Gayle would have a simple childhood, where she wouldn't even know about magic. She wouldn't know about her destiny and the fact that she would be wearing a crown one day.

Until her eighteenth birthday she would be normal. Human. Then her parents would tell her the truth and she would be brought to Saluverus. To learn about her magic, and to train for whatever threat she was born to face. With the Asters by her side.

That would be next month. Only four weeks left and then she would come to Saluverus. The miracle reincarnation herself. The Queen. The wolf. The *Bhediya*, as Aiyana had preferred to be called; the Hindi word for wolf.

Sky could see the hope and joy in Sophie's eyes. They were the Aster generation that would write history. Never before, and maybe never again, had Queen Aiyana's magic returned to the earth. And they would be fighting alongside it.

"Don't get your hopes up," Sky told his sister.

Sophie looked up at him. "I won't."

Her words weren't convincing. "One month, one week. Either way, she'll be here before you know it," Sky said.

Sophie's eyes sparkled. "Can you imagine?"

Sky grinned at his sister. In these moments he couldn't believe how fierce and deadly she could be on a battle field. Sure, she looked disgusting now, with tangled hair falling out of her plait and blood on her face, but there was a childish joy in her that she rarely ever showed. The prospect of Gayle Mendosa coming had brought it out in her.

The Asters entered the Board Room minutes later. It was a spacious room, with a heavy, round, oak table in the middle. A corner desk filled up most of one of the short walls and part of a longer one. Two large computer screens were on top, next to piles and piles of paperwork that Sky never wanted to ask about, in case he would be asked to read through any of it. The other long wall was completely covered with filing cabinets, and under the window, along the last short end, stood a large chest of drawers. Despite all the furniture, the room was large enough for at least twenty people to stand around without feeling claustrophobic. The oak table stood quite isolated in the centre of the room.

Instinctively the Asters took their seats at the oak table.

Axel Reed was already there. He was a large man, with broad shoulders and big arms. He had a round face with blonde hair that was cut extremely short. Sky couldn't remember the last time he had seen Axel smile. He always had a stern and serious look on his face, and the large, badly healed scar near his right temple only made him more intimidating. He was Saluverus' Ambassador, and the boss of everyone in the room.

Axel wasn't the only Ambassador in the world. Back in Aiyana's reign, the Queen had created two other islands like Saluverus: one in the South Atlantic Ocean off the coast of Namibia called Auro, and one in the Indian Ocean off the coast of Indonesia called Viria. Lastly Aiyana had created an undetectable place high in the mountains south of Russia, called Glacialis. Also known as the Frozen Dungeons, it was a prison land where captured and interrogated Disciples spent the rest of their days. Glacialis was also home to the weapon's factories and a laboratory complex, and a small village housing the people who worked there. Every single weapon the Asters and Affinites worked and trained with was developed and made there.

All three of those places had their own Ambassador, but Axel Reed outranked them all. His job made him, while being just an Affinite and possessing no magic, one of the most powerful people in the world.

He stood with his back towards the Asters as he leaned on the chest of drawers and looked out of the window to the island below.

Sylvia Allen was also in the room, standing near Axel by the edge of the window. She was a short, slightly round woman with grey hair and light eyes. For reasons Sky couldn't begin to care about, but always picked up on, Sylvia always wore some form of clothing depicting any kind of flower. Sylvia was Saluverus' Consul, and was in charge of all Saluverus' internal affairs.

The other two people Sky had expected to be in the room were also there. Felix Hauser and Nicholas Nelson: the Spymaster and the Emissary. Nicholas, the African-American Emissary originally from Texas, United States, was in contact with every Affinite who didn't live on one of the three islands. The only Affinites that he wasn't in contact with were the Watchers, who were special agents in Felix's service, and the Mergers. Also working for Felix, Mergers were spy-Affinites who went undercover into the Underworld and integrated into the life of Disciples to feed any information they could find on the Kings and their movements back to Felix.

The four adults in the room and Jackson Kelly as Commanding Chief, made up the Small Council, and made every major decision that had anything to do with the Asters.

Once the Asters took their seats and Jackson Kelly had closed the door behind him, Axel Reed turned around. Sky noticed the remote control the Ambassador held in his hand.

"Thank you for coming," Axel said, his voice deep and strong.

The Asters nodded in silence.

"As you know, Gayle Mendosa's arrival on Saluverus is planned for four weeks' time. That has not changed," the Ambassador continued.

Sky glanced at Sophie. She didn't show her disappointment one bit. Her thunderstorm grey eyes were focused as she listened intently.

"But the Underworld knows her age, too. If you would all look at the screen." Axel held up his hand and pressed a button on the remote control.

The Asters turned their heads and watched the television screen, that hung above the short end of the corner desk, turn on. It showed an image that Sky had seen a hundred times. It was a world map, covered in blue and black dots. The blue dots represented every living Affinite on the earth's surface, while each black dot represented a Dark Disciple. Or at least, these were the locations and the number of Disciples *detected* on the Surface of the earth.

"Crap," Sky heard Matu mutter under his breath.

Sky thought the same thing.

All across the world, on every continent, there were many more black spots than Sky had ever seen before. Most Disciples spent their lives in the Underworld, serving one of the seven Higher Kings in one of their Underworld domains. They often ventured up onto the Surface, and, if need be, the Asters could be sent in to bring one back for questioning. Or, if the Disciples were stirring up any kind of trouble, the Asters were allowed to capture them and send them off to the Frozen Dungeons; or kill them, if they were really posing a threat.

Sky had never seen so many Disciples on the Surface before. And it wasn't hard to figure out who they were all looking for: Gayle Mendosa.

Axel turned back to the Asters. "We know that seventeen years ago, a captured Affinite told one of the Kings that Gayle would not be brought up on Saluverus, but on one of the continents, and without any knowledge of her magic. They didn't learn Gayle's location from the

Affinite because she didn't know it; as you know, only a select few do. In the first months of Gayle's life the Surface was just as densely filled with Disciples as it is now. The Kings wanted to find her, raise her as their own, and harness her magic for their own destructive ambitions. Sporadically over the last eighteen years they have attempted to find her. Before you came of age, we sent your parents in to stop them on those occasions." Axel took a short breath. "But the Disciples are active again, and will not be scared so easily back to the Underworld this time around. We don't need to capture and interrogate one to know what their orders are: find Gayle's location before she is brought here and starts her training to become, not only the strongest creature in the world, but also our Queen."

Axel turned his gaze from the Asters to the television screen. "From their distribution across the world it looks for the moment that they still have no idea of where the Mendosas are."

The Asters remained silent as the Ambassador spoke. Sky didn't know Gayle's precise location—none of the Asters did. Only the Small Council and Sky's mother knew where she had grown up for the last eighteen years. The Small Council had preferred none of the Asters of that generation to know, but Madeleine Mayne had insisted that her transporting shimmer could get her and the other Asters there in seconds if something were to go wrong, and it could be too late if the emergency call had to go through the Small Council first.

"Why not bring her in sooner?" Matu asked. "Every day you don't we risk her being found."

Axel nodded, acknowledging the question. "Because the world right now is a magical minefield. There are detectors everywhere, and the second any Aster magic is used near the Mendosas, their cloaking magic will fail them and they can be found. We will be using the next four weeks to prepare for Gayle and her parents' journey here with as little risk as possible. We will, for example, be making sure the airpaths are clear from any tampering, so that a shimmer can pass through with no detection and no interference."

"So, why are we here?" Sky asked in a bored tone. He eyed what seemed like millions of black dots on the world map. "You can't expect us to capture or kill every one of those Disciples." Though Sky would love to try...

Sylvia Allen came up to stand beside Axel. Her warm smile was a stark contrast to Axel's cold stare. "We're not."

Axel looked at Sky directly. "The Disciples don't know that outside of this room only *your mother* knows Gayle Mendosa's precise location. We expect that the search they've been on for the past weeks will soon stop, and that they will use other, more direct, means. From this moment you are now on strict orders to rest when you can, as much as you can. Because any second, any Disciple can turn violent in their desperation to find Gayle Mendosa before it is too late."

Axel turned away from Sky and looked at each of the other Asters in turn. "And you need to be ready for when they do."

Chapter 4

When Axel had warned the Asters that they could be summoned at any second, Sophie hadn't really expected it to be that same night.

At two in the morning.

Sophie shot out of bed the second the chip in her arm started buzzing.

Every Aster had a chip implanted in their upper right arm. They were a mix of technology and magic that allowed the Asters to be tracked and their well-being monitored during a mission. And when they weren't on a mission it was used to summon them *for* one.

Within seconds Sophie was wearing her loose fighting trousers, stretch top and leather jacket. She was tying her hair into a plait as she stepped out of her room and into the common room. The Asters lived in the top half of one of the bigger circular towers of the castle. Divided over two floors were six bedrooms and a small common room. Sophie, Lian and Nathan's bedrooms were on the bottom floor, while Sky's, Matu's and a third empty room were on the second floor. A narrow staircase spiralled up to a balcony, which gave access to the three bedrooms on the second floor. The common room contained two deep red sofas and a lounge chair that encircled a large fire. Against the only free stretch of wall stood a large bookcase made of dark wood. A thick, patterned rug covered most of the stone flooring.

Sophie looked up to see Sky practically jump out of his bedroom and onto the balcony. His face was flushed and his eyes were sparkling.

Sophie didn't want to ask why. The two nodded at each other once, when a second later the other three bedroom doors opened and Matu, Nathan and Lian stepped out. All dressed in the same fighting gear and leather jackets, the five Asters made their way to the centre of the common room. They stood in a circle and held each other's hands while Sky's Band started pulsing blue and the five of them shimmered.

Once the blue light vanished from Sophie's eyesight, she found herself standing in the Board Room. Only Sylvia Allen, the island's Consul, was there. She and the other members of the Small Council had interchangeable nightshifts so that there was always someone to call on the Asters in case of an emergency.

Without saying anything yet, the Asters moved quickly to the oak table in the middle of the room. Each of their signature weapons lay on top of it. There was a closet in the back of the room filled with weapons for whenever the Asters were sent on a mission. Whoever was on duty at the time would lay them out on the oak table while the Asters made their way to the Board Room.

Sophie strapped on her belt from which her rapier hung in its sheath and pulled the miniature cross bow over her left hand. Lian grabbed his bow and quiver, and took a simple sword as well. Sky picked up his short spear and sheathed another two short swords to the outside of his thighs, while Matu took a single dagger in addition to his knuckle knives, and Nathan strapped his two broadswords to his back.

While the Asters were getting ready, Sylvia explained to them why they had been called in. "An emergency call has come in from the Okoth family in Nairobi, Kenya."

"What?" Matu snapped round to face Sylvia. "Are they all right?"

Sophie didn't bother to glance at her brother. Now was not the time to be concerned, even if any of them knew the family personally. If Matu wasn't up for whatever they might face, he should stay behind. Matu knew it, and was rational enough to pull back if necessary.

Sophie knew that the Okoth family consisted of Reth and Eidi Okoth, and their thirteen-year-old son Yaro. Reth and Matu's father had been friends for years. They had trained together on Saluverus ever since they were children, before they both moved back to their home town, Nairobi. Sophie knew Reth was like a second father to Matu. When he had returned to Nairobi, Reth had taken over the main Affinite training programme in the city, and was always in close contact with Jackson Kelly and the other members of the Small Council about the progress of the Affinites training with him.

"I have no more information other than the signal. I have tried to call, but with no answer. You are to go there immediately to see what has happened. Expect anything," Sylvia answered. She looked at Matu for a moment. "Are you all right to go?"

Matu gave a short nod. Sophie expected nothing less. Matu was always the calm, calculating, rational one. He would be able to separate his personal feelings and possible fear from the mission. Maybe not as well as Nathan, but not even Sophie understood exactly how Nathan could turn from warm and kind to cold and clinical like flipping a switch.

Sylvia nodded too, then turned her attention to the television screen still showing the map of the world. Saluverus' Consul pressed a button on the remote, which caused the map to zoom in on Africa, then to Kenya, then to Nairobi, and then even closer to one of the streets. "Good. Now as you can see, there are no Disciples at the house, but they can arrive while you are there. Be careful and be on the alert. Find out anything you can. Now go."

Sophie turned to Sky. Her brother didn't need any other order than that. No sooner had Sylvia spoken the last word than the blue light filled Sophie's vision and the five Asters shimmered from Saluverus.

The second the blue light vanished the Asters found themselves standing in a dark living room.

Matu glanced out through the nearest window and found that it was just as dark here as it had been on Saluverus. He knew it was around four o'clock in the morning here, two hours later than where they had come from. He had visited his parents often enough to know the time difference. It was strange to think that his parents were asleep not so far away from here.

Matu looked around him. He had been in this very living room many times before, but never had it looked like this. Even though the lights were off, Matu could see by the moonlight that a struggle had taken place. Knowing exactly where the light switch was that would turn on the lamp on the ceiling, Matu took two steps to his right and reached behind him.

Nothing happened as he flipped the switch. Matu tried again, but nothing changed.

"The lights won't come on," Matu said. He could just about make out who was who in the darkness.

"Classic," Sky mumbled.

One by one, torches illuminated the living room. It was a small space; Reth had never been one for luxury. As long as they had a kitchen to cook in, a sofa to sit on, and a bed to sleep in, he hadn't cared what his house looked like. He spent most of his time in the training centre, anyway. Eidi had been the one to ensure that they didn't live in a hut, but in a house with three small bedrooms with a warm feel to it.

For Yaro and for visitors, she had said.

Matu couldn't smile at the memory as his torchlight danced over the discarded books on the sofa and the floor. Everything that had been on the shelves above the sofa, including a potted plant, had been violently swept off. The rug had also been tossed aside and the small coffee table had been flipped over. The cushions from the sofa had been thrown everywhere; they were sliced open and the stuffing was all over the place.

"We'll check upstairs," Sophie said. No one disagreed when she and Nathan headed up the stairs.

Matu continued to shine his torchlight through the living room. Knowing that something bad had happened here, the place suddenly had a different feel to it. The air seemed to stick to his skin and the shadows had a more sinister look to them. Matu tried to keep his breathing under control as he spotted drops of blood on the floor. He forced himself to keep calm and continue to survey the living room. The small television in the corner had been turned upside down and the little table it used to stand on had its drawers pulled out, and they, too, were lying on the floor, their contents scattered.

"Matu..."

The alarm in Sky's voice had Matu dreading to turn around. When he did, and pointed his torch in Sky's direction, his breath hitched.

He was in motion before he had even thought of moving his legs. A second later he was standing over the body of a woman, lying face-down. Sky was kneeling at her waist, fingers at her wrist. There was blood pooling all around her middle, and she lay there as still as death.

The woman didn't need to be turned around for Matu to know that this was Eidi Okoth, Reth's wife and Yaro's mother. He recognised the delicate frame, the shape of her hands and the style of her hair.

There was blood surrounding her head as well, but not nearly as much as around her abdomen. Matu glanced at Sky who had his eyes closed as he searched for the woman's pulse.

"Sophie!" Matu yelled.

Sky lifted his head up from the body. The light in his always so lively blue eyes seemed to have gone out as he shook his head.

"No..." Matu whispered. He didn't look up as he heard footsteps on the staircase behind him. All he could think about was the woman lying before him. The woman who had always been so kind to him. Who had such a brilliant smile it lit up her entire face, and who, as human, had accepted her Affinite husband and the magical, dangerous world he came from with fascination and pure openness. She didn't deserve this.

"What are you—oh God..." Sophie said as she realised what Matu, Sky and Lian were all standing around.

"She's dead," Matu said softly.

At that moment Nathan also re-appeared from upstairs.

"No sign of anyone up there?" Lian asked before Nathan could form any words about Eidi's death.

Nathan tore his eyes away from the body in their midst and shook his head. "No, no one."

Matu clenched his fists. "Then where are Reth and Yaro?" he demanded.

Lian laid a hand on Matu's shoulder. "We'll find them."

Matu loosed a deep breath and closed his eyes. Yes, they would find Eidi's husband and son. They owed that to her. They had to, because they hadn't been fast enough to save her.

Sophie knelt down at Eidi's head. Her long, dark and frizzy hair reached halfway down her back. Sophie leaned over, and as she lifted some of the hair away from Eidi's face Sophie's hand stilled.

"What the..." she whispered. With her other hand she angled her torch in such a way that the woman's face was suddenly bathed in light.

"Turn her over," Sophie snapped.

Matu frowned.

"What?" Sky said.

"*Turn her over,*" Sophie repeated more sharply.

Sky didn't ask again as he leaned over and started to turn over the body.

Matu helped him. "What's going on?"

"She's not dead."

"What? But I—" Sky started.

"You're a dumbass, that's what. Get out of my way." Sophie didn't even look up as she continued. "Lian, keep an eye out, make sure we're still alone here."

And then Matu saw it, too. As they rolled the body over there was a tiny flutter of Eidi's lashes and a slow movement of her eyes as she realised what was happening to her.

If that movement had given Matu hope, the sight of the front of Eidi's body ripped it all away again. Her whole belly had been sliced open from side to side, and part of her small intestines were hanging out.

Sky was about to reach them to help Sophie put them back into her body when Sophie snapped again, "*Don't!*"

Nathan, who was about to help as well, looked alarmed, and froze. "I'll stand watch, too," he said. The icy calm of a mission had descended upon him again, and there was nothing visible of the insecure, sweet boy now as he stood up gracefully and moved to stand near the closest window.

"Is there anything we can do?" Sky asked.

"Not you, no," Sophie breathed. "I just need to be fast enough."

The Band around her wrist was glowing a golden colour. The light spread to her own hands before she started picking up the intestines and carefully put them back in Eidi's body.

"But—" Sky started.

"If you'd paid more attention in class than to girls," Sophie interrupted dispassionately as she methodically worked her way around Eidi's open abdomen, "you would know that my magic disinfects my hands." There was utter focus in her eyes as she worked. "Your hands are not clean. Even if you could help put them back in, which, unless you ever paid attention in medical class you wouldn't even know how to properly, your dirty hands would give her an infection. And then that would kill her."

Sophie didn't look up as she spoke. If it hadn't been for the tense situation and Eidi's life on the line, Matu would've laughed at Sophie's disparaging comments about Sky's reputation back when they had been at school.

"That was low," Sky muttered.

"Yeah, well, so were your grades."

Sky snorted.

"Will you both shut it?" Matu snapped.

Eidi loosed a raspy breath.

"Talk to her," Sophie commanded, looking up at Matu. Sky quickly stepped back, making sure his torch was still aimed at Eidi's stomach, so Matu could take his place by her side.

Matu didn't want to stop looking at what Sophie was doing. He knew that she was working as fast as she could and that she wouldn't fail, yet he still wanted to make sure. Still, he tore his eyes away and met Eidi's. The poor woman's face was a mask of excruciating pain. Her brow was covered in sweat, and it mixed with the blood from the thin gash across her forehead. The delicate hand Matu now clamped within his own massive one was clammy and incredibly weak. She barely held on to him.

Matu started soothing Eidi in their native language, the Swahili words coming softly and rhythmically; telling her whatever she needed to hear to hold on. He told her that Sophie was the best, though Eidi knew damn well who Sophie was and what she could do. Matu assured her he had no doubt Eidi would walk out of there in no time.

Though that only seemed to make Eidi's fear grow.

Matu snapped his head up to Nathan and Lian. "Search this house. Find something, *anything*, that might tell you where Reth and Yaro are. *NOW!*"

But before either Aster could move, Eidi rasped, "No…"

Matu looked back down. "What?"

At that moment Eidi grasped his hand tightly and screamed. It pierced the deafening silence of the night. Matu snapped his head over to Sophie in horror.

"Soph!"

But her hands were glowing brightly. Her eyes were still fixated on them. Matu couldn't see any of Eidi's intestines anymore and he watched as the skin of her belly started knitting itself back together. A few seconds later Eidi's skin showed no sign of there ever being such a life-threatening injury. The blood staining her dark skin, her clothes, the floor and Sophie's hands, was the only evidence that, if the Asters had arrived only minutes later, Eidi would've been dead.

Eidi Okoth took one gulp of air and shot up to a sitting position. She would've fallen back down again if Matu hadn't steadied her with an arm at her back. His Band glowed bronze for a moment, but his magic settled again. He didn't need his magic of Strength to keep this woman upright. Eidi turned to him and squeezed his other hand. The gash along her forehead had vanished too. Only dried blood remained. Then, remembering what had happened, her free hand shot to her mouth, and she started crying.

"It's all right," Sophie soothed, the earlier sharpness in her voice having vanished. "Deep breaths."

"What happened here?" Matu asked.

"Disciples," Eidi breathed as she turned her attention back to Matu. And then the whole story came out. Along with a rush of tears that streamed down her cheeks.

"They knew about our training programme for all Affinites in the country. They knew our connection to the Small Council. They thought, because of that, we knew Gayle Mendosa's location."

Matu's heart sank as Eidi Okoth continued her story.

"They cut all the wires—all the lights. We heard them, but we couldn't see anything. And they pulled us out of bed. There were so many... so many... And they tied me to a chair—Reth, too. And they hurt..." Her voice hitched, and she choked, "They hurt Yaro."

Eidi sobbed greatly before continuing. "They thought we'd tell them if they promised not to touch Yaro, but we didn't know... Neither of us knew... They didn't believe us..."

"Where is Yaro? And Reth? Where are they now?" Matu pushed. He held his right hand steady at her back while gently stroking her left hand with his thumb.

"They took them. I don't know where exactly. Because Reth owns and runs the Academy, and I am just human, they thought there was a better chance he'd know the Queen's location than me. So they told him they'd kill me and that Yaro would be next if he didn't give them the information. But he doesn't have it... neither of us know... Oh, Matu... They attacked me, and left me for dead, and they took them both. I don't know what they will do to Yaro to get Reth to speak, but Reth doesn't know... You have to go after them! Please, you have to save them!"

"Shh," Matu assured her as Eidi continued working herself up. "We'll find them, I promise. We'll do all we can to find them."

"But you can't be here while we look," Sophie pointed out.

Eidi stared at Sophie without responding.

Sky backed up his sister. "Sophie's right. You won't be safe here."

"They're right," Matu whispered. Eidi turned her head slowly back to Matu. Her body trembling violently, Eidi nodded slowly.

Matu nodded to the rest of them and started helping Eidi back to her feet. Despite the woman's shaking, Eidi stood stronger than Matu had expected. She was an amazing human.

"Send Lian, me and Eidi back," Matu instructed Sky. "She needs to get to the Medical Bay and we will update Sylvia. You three find out what you can about this attack. See if you can find anything that can tell us which Disciples did this. That might narrow down our search in the Underworld." For the Underworld was divided up into territories, and while the seven Higher Kings rarely ventured into the territory of another, it could cost Reth and Yaro their lives if the Asters stormed the wrong one. Knowing which King the Disciples responsible for this served, would already help focus the search.

Then maybe, if the Asters were lucky enough to find anything more specific, they could find Reth and Yaro before that specific King discovered that Reth had no idea where to find Gayle Mendosa.

Chapter 5

Axel Reed and Emissary Nicholas Nelson had joined Sylvia Allen in the Board Room while the Asters were away on their mission. Axel and Sylvia had both taken a seat at the large oak table, while Nicholas was typing furiously behind the computer as Matu and Lian shimmered in with Eidi Okoth between them.

Sylvia got up the second she laid eyes on the blood-soaked Kenyan woman.

"Eidi!" the Consul exclaimed.

Eidi Okoth, still in shock from the events of earlier that night, barely acknowledged the Consul as Matu led her to one of the chairs at the table.

Nicholas stared at the woman. As Emissary of Saluverus he knew about every Affinite in the world, as did the two Emissaries from Viria and Auro. However, he was in closer contact with the Affinites who served a direct purpose to the Small Council. The Okoth family, because their training Academy was the largest in Kenya, were always in contact with both Jackson Kelly and Nicholas Nelson. They would speak often about the progress of the Affinites in the Academy, since every Affinite would be asked to take a place in the army should a war ever break out. This had been taken all the more seriously in the past ten years because of Gayle's magic, and the promise of the great threat that her magical birth portended.

"I'll get some water," Sylvia was saying, and the woman bustled out of the Board Room.

Nicholas watched silently as Eidi, with her eyes closed, focused on breathing as steadily as possible. Yet the tears that rolled down her cheeks and the shaking of her hands showed she was in no way calm. Or in any state to tell the members of the Small Council who were still in the room what had happened that night.

"Where are the others?" Axel asked, filling the silence.

"Still in Nairobi," Matu answered, looking up from Eidi. "Sky shimmered us here for Eidi's protection."

"What happened to her?" Axel asked.

"Disciples meant to kill her. If we'd got there any later she wouldn't have survived her wounds. Sophie healed her just in time," Matu explained. He left out the debacle of Sky's initial diagnosis; Matu was still seething inwardly about what that could have meant for Eidi.

The door opened again and Sylvia entered with a glass of water in one hand, and a jug in the other. She set the jug on the corner desk and walked over to Eidi. The woman raised her eyes and with a shaky hand took the glass Sylvia offered her. The water in the glass trembled as Eidi raised it to her lips to drink.

"They meant to kill her?" Axel asked.

"She should've already been dead. The Disciples didn't check that she was when they left," Lian explained.

It seemed strange to be talking about Eidi's death so lightly when the woman was sitting right in front of them. But Eidi didn't seem to be any more distraught than she already was while the Ambassador continued his questions.

"Why would they be that sloppy?" Axel asked, suspiciously.

"Because it was no longer about her," Matu answered.

"Reth and Yaro?"

It was the first time Nicholas had spoken since Matu and Lian had shimmered into the room. He was looking at Eidi as he asked the question.

"Are the others still in Nairobi to find them?" the Emissary added.

Lian shook his head. "The Disciples took both of them."

"They believe Reth knows Gayle Mendosa's location. They tortured Yaro first, to see if either Eidi or Reth would break. When they were sure Eidi didn't know anything, they killed her and took Reth and Yaro away. Or *tried* to kill her," Matu finished explaining.

Axel swore under his breath.

"They think Reth might know?" Nicholas asked.

"Given his high status with the Small Council, it's not the strangest thing to presume," Sylvia said.

"But he doesn't know," Lian said.

"We know that," Axel snarled. The sound of his voice sent shivers up Matu's spine. He and Lian both knew that the anger emanating from the Ambassador wasn't directed at them, but at the information they were giving.

Matu clenched his fists by his side. He forced himself to keep his mouth shut even when he wanted to demand how they were going to get Reth and Yaro back. But he would never demand that of Axel Reed. The Small Council would come with a plan once they'd had time to process all the information, and Matu and the other Asters would just have to wait until that happened.

Lian didn't have that kind of patience. Not when it came to saving people who were in trouble. "And *what* are we going to do to make sure he doesn't get killed when they find that out?"

Matu shot his brother a warning look but Lian wasn't looking at him.

Axel opened his mouth to speak, and Matu braced himself for the Ambassador's anger. But before any words came, Axel was cut off.

"They're... they're going to kill Yaro," Eidi stammered. Her shaking had increased and she looked even paler than before.

"Get her out of here," Axel commanded.

Sylvia stepped in front of Eidi, and said softly, "We're not going to let that happen, all right?"

Sylvia took Eidi's hands and raised the woman up to her feet.

"Take her to the Medical Bay for observation," Axel ordered.

"Sophie healed her," Lian said. "Physically she's fine."

"She's still in shock," Sylvia responded sharply. "We need to keep an eye on her until she calms down." She softened her voice again and directed it towards Eidi. "That's right, come with me now."

Sylvia wrapped an arm around Eidi and guided her out of the Board Room. At the door Eidi struggled to loosen Sylvia's grip on her so that she could turn around. For just that moment her trembling stopped as she stared back at the Ambassador.

"Save Yaro," the woman said, her voice stronger than any one of them would have expected. "If you have to choose, you save Yaro. Reth would want that, too."

Sylvia returned an arm around Eidi and tried to guide her out of the room. "Don't talk like that. We are not faced with such a choice yet."

But Eidi wouldn't have it. She shook Sylvia off again. She looked at both Matu and Lian and said, "If you do have to make that choice, make this one."

"Get some rest Mrs. Okoth." Axel spoke before either Matu or Lian could open their mouths.

Eidi looked back at the Ambassador. "*Promise me,*" she pushed.

Axel stared the woman down for a moment. Yet Eidi was unflinching. "Promise me," she whispered hoarsely, with the last of her strength.

After a moment all Axel gave was a short nod. Eidi wouldn't get more of a response from the Ambassador than that and she knew it. The Kenyan woman nodded slowly. She dropped her head and her hands resumed their shaking. She let Sylvia put an arm around her once more and together they left the Board Room.

The door closed behind them with a soft click. Everyone left in the room stared at it in silence, until Nicholas said, "Let's hope it doesn't come to that."

"Agreed," Axel said gruffly. The Ambassador turned to the two Asters standing in the room. "The others are trying to find any indication of which King those Disciples work for, correct?"

"Yes, but I don't think—" Matu started. His words were cut off by the appearance of a blue light in the middle of the Board Room. Matu and Lian both took a step back as Sophie, Sky and Nathan appeared in the room.

Sophie looked absolutely horrible. Not only were her hands and clothes covered in Eidi's blood, but the dark liquid had somehow also managed to stain parts of her face and blonde hair.

Matu's heart sank as he took in their faces. The grave expressions on them told him enough: they hadn't found anything that would lead them to a specific King, and therefore a specific territory in the Underworld. It would be nearly impossible to find Yaro and Reth when they didn't even know where to start looking. Even if they did manage to capture the right Disciple who would break under interrogation and tell them what they needed to know, they might already be too late. It wouldn't be long before the Disciples found out that Reth had no idea where Gayle Mendosa was, and Matu didn't want to think about what would happen when they did. Disciples, and certainly Kings, weren't ones to let captured Affinites walk out free once they had foregone their usefulness.

If Matu had any say in the matter he would go into the African Underworld and start there. Disciples had no magic, and couldn't transport. The odds that Reth and Yaro had been taken by Disciples from another territory were small. It had happened in the past that Disciples from one King ventured into the territory of another, but not for many years. Matu would bet anything that the African King was behind this, and he wanted to start looking for Reth right now.

But it wasn't up to him.

It was up to Axel and the rest of the Small Council. And Matu would await their decision and follow their orders. Even if he didn't agree with them. Even if he couldn't stop picturing Reth and Yaro's faces in the back of his mind. The thought of his father's best friend being held somewhere in the Underworld, his own life not being threatened, but that of his thirteen-year-old son... It made Matu sick to even think about it.

And yet he still wouldn't do anything rash.

It wasn't his call to make, and it wasn't his way to disobey orders.

"Nothing?" Axel asked, reading the same thing on the faces of the three Asters who had just shimmered in.

Sky shook his head, his eyes blazing. He looked as though he wanted to grab one of the chairs around the oak table and throw it across the room in anger. Though he seemed arrogant and nonchalant to the rest of the world, and to the other Asters ninety per cent of the time, it was in these moments when his real self shone through. His feeling of uselessness angered him more than anything, especially with his goal to remain known as the greatest Aster of his generation. He wasn't ready to say that there was nothing he could do. Sky would rip through the whole Underworld if that's what it took to get Reth and Yaro out.

That was the main difference between Matu and Sky. The anger that shone in Sky's eyes was the same as the anger Matu felt; Matu was just better at hiding it and controlling it. He would keep it to himself. It wasn't his job to get emotional about Affinite victims. It was his job to save them when he was ordered to. And not a second sooner.

"Reth and Yaro won't be killed just yet. The Disciples need Reth alive to tell them Gayle Mendosa's location," Nathan said matter-of-factly. The cool, focused calm that took over Nathan when on a mission apparently hadn't left him yet. There was no emotion in his voice as he spoke.

"But how long until they figure out that Reth doesn't know?" Lian asked. Matu detected the edge in Lian's voice, but his body language revealed nothing. Lian also couldn't stand waiting around, but not in the same way Sky did. Sky's reasons were more selfish; wanting to prove he and his magic could handle anything. Lian couldn't stand being ordered to wait and do nothing ever since he had received that exact same order when his parents had perished in a house fire one year earlier, when he thought there was still something that could've been done. Matu knew it would weigh on Lian's conscience that two Affinites were out there, helpless, and the Asters were ordered not to go in and help immediately.

Nicholas cleared his throat. "There is no way to know for certain. What we do know is that they won't stop with Reth when they do find out."

Sky grunted in acknowledgment of the truth of these words and stepped away from his siblings. He moved to the window and leaned on the chest of drawers standing underneath it. He remained silent as he stared out into the darkness beyond, his frustration clearly visible in his body language.

"So literally every Affinite on the Surface is in danger?" Sophie asked sharply.

There was a knock on the door. It opened and Felix Hauser stepped inside. Axel nodded to the Spymaster and turned back to Sophie. "Not all of them. Kings and Disciples have information on us just like we have information on them. They will know which Affinites have the largest chance of having information on Gayle Mendosa. It looks like the attack on the Okoths was the first move in this strategy."

While Axel spoke Felix walked over to where Nicholas was sitting, and leaned against the desk.

"But none of them know!" Sophie exclaimed. "How are we supposed to protect all of them until Gayle gets here?"

"By not having to do it alone." Axel nodded towards Felix and continued. "All Watchers on the Surface will be re-directed to cover the houses of Affinites who are at highest risk. We were lucky with Eidi Okoth. If the Disciples hadn't made the mistake of leaving her alive she wouldn't have been able to sound the alarm."

Matu looked up at this. "Eidi did that? How could she have done anything to notify the Small Council in the state she was in?"

"There was an alarm button on the underside of the dining table. It works on an independent battery, so it still worked when the wires were cut. She must have pressed it after Yaro and Reth were taken. The Disciples were smart: they attacked in such a way that neither Reth nor Eidi had the time to press the emergency button behind the headboard of their bed. If they hadn't left her alive it would have taken longer for us to find her, and to work out what happened," Axel explained. "We were lucky."

Four of the Asters were momentarily speechless as they registered the bravery and strength it had taken Eidi to do what she had done. Under other circumstances Sky might also have given thought to this, but not right now. Now he was still too wound up with frustration.

"You can't use the word *lucky* when two Affinites, including *a kid*, are being tortured as we speak," Sky growled from the window.

Axel ignored him. "If Disciples attack other important Affinite families, which we're expecting they will, those families might not be able to send us a signal during or after the attack like Eidi Okoth did. Hence, Felix's Watchers. They will watch, but they will not engage. They will call on us, and we will call on you. The Watchers will only engage if they think the Affinites are in real danger of being taken away and down into the Underworld. Until then, they are to observe only, and pick up whatever they can about the Disciples and from which Underworld territory they came from."

"Won't they just be from Africa?" Lian asked. "What are the odds that they came from anywhere else?"

Axel turned to look at him. "That mistake has been made by Ambassadors before me. I will not be making the same mistake."

Lian curled his lip, but before he could say anything more, Sky had turned around from the window. "Okay, fine. Say they're not from the African Underworld. What if there is another attack and those *Watchers* don't learn where they come from?"

Felix Hauser narrowed his eyes at Sky's pronunciation of *Watchers*. His Austrian-German accent was thick through his English as he spoke. "They will. *You* know that Disciples can be recognised by the distinctive clothing or weaponry of the King they serve. But there are other signs. My men and women have been trained to recognise even the smallest tells. They will know which King is initiating these attacks, and from there, you will know from where to rescue Reth and Yaro."

Sky narrowed his eyes as well. "*If* they're still alive to be rescued."

"What about the other Affinites?" Sophie interjected, before any other words could be exchanged between the already livid Sky and the Spymaster. "Surely you don't have enough Watchers to cover every single important Affinite house. Many families have ties with the Small Council. I'm sure the Disciples' intel won't be so precise as to know which family could know what, exactly."

Her knowledge was shining through. Matu waited for Felix's answer as Sophie's Band pulsed golden. From where he was standing, Matu could see the symbol on her wrist that made her magic different to his or that of any other Aster: the staff of Caduceus, the healing staff, representing her magic of Health and Knowledge.

She was using her magic of knowledge now, her memory and her brilliance working side by side, calculating exactly what risks there were to keeping the Affinites out in the world instead of safely behind the Curtain of either one of the three undetectable islands. She knew as well as Matu did that they couldn't call for a world-wide evacuation of the Surface; not after just a single attack.

But she also knew that what had happened to the Okoth family would most certainly happen again, because Reth didn't have the information the Disciples sought. Matu didn't blame Sky for not trusting Felix's Watchers to protect an Affinite family during an attack until the Asters arrived. They were spies and not soldiers for a reason. And from the looks of Eidi, and the remaining blood that had been on the floor in the Okoth living room, these Disciples knew a thing or two about violence and fighting.

Felix looked over to Axel. The Asters turned to the Ambassador, too, and waited for him to speak, but it was Nicholas, the Emissary, who spoke first.

"We're sending out a protocol. Every Affinite family on the Surface, even those under the protection of Felix's Watchers, will send in a signal every evening at ten o'clock, their time, to let us know that they are alright and untouched. Our technology will be able to tell us from which families we should hear something at what time. This way we can keep tabs on each and every Affinite family and their well-being."

"That still would have us acting *after* something has already happened," Lian pointed out. Again his body language revealed nothing but calm energy, but there was a slight sharpness to his voice.

"At the moment there is nothing more we can do," Axel replied.

"Yeah, right," Sky breathed softly, turning back to look outside.

Axel glared at the boy at the window, but Sky didn't meet Axel's frown. He continued to stare out into the darkness.

"We will warn the families and allow them to come to one of the three islands if they wish. We will explain the situation and how large the chance is that what happened to the Okoth family will happen to them. If they choose to remain where they are, the protocols of the ten o'clock signal, and Felix's Watchers, will be what we go by," Axel said clearly.

The Ambassador looked around the room, his eyes resting on each and every Aster before continuing. "Thank you for responding so quickly."

"Not quickly enough," Sky muttered.

"ENOUGH!" Axel thundered through the room. Even Sky recoiled at the outburst. He didn't apologise, however.

Matu watched as his brother and the Ambassador glared at each other. Their anger came from the same place: they hated being too late, and not being able to do any more than they had already done. You would think they could work together very well, considering their shared desires. However, they always seemed to have different ideas when it came to the protection of the Affinites and of keeping the Kings from reclaiming the Surface of the earth. Matu had lost track of how many meetings had ended with Sky muttering his disagreement to himself and Axel shouting to shut him up.

Axel's eyes were still on Sky as he spoke with such a dangerous calm that the hairs on Matu's arms stood up. You could cut the tension in the room with a knife.

"You have done all that you could tonight. Every hour it is ten p.m. somewhere else in the world, and if we get no word, you will be sent to investigate. Get some sleep while you can. You're all dismissed."

Sky was still tightly wound as he and the other Asters walked through the castle. He rolled his shoulders in an attempt to relieve some of the tension, and very slowly the muscles in his neck and back started to relax.

Beside him, Sophie had started yawning. Sky looked around him and saw the fatigue in all his siblings' eyes. The cold, strong demeanour

Nathan always had during training and missions had also left him when they had stepped out of the Board Room, and he now, too, walked with his shoulders hunched and his head down. Sky himself, however, couldn't be more awake. Sure, Axel said there was nothing more they could do.

He was wrong.

There was.

There was always *something* they could do.

For starters they could bring Gayle Mendosa to the island early. The Disciples weren't going to stop going after Affinites who might have the information of their future Queen's location. Once word got out that Gayle was safely on Saluverus, the attacks on the important Affinite families would stop; that much seemed to be inevitable.

But that still left Reth and Yaro somewhere in the Underworld, and they would die the second word got out that Gayle was safely behind Saluverus' Curtain. Sky had refrained from asking Axel what they were to do about the captured father and son. The way the Ambassador had told them they were dismissed had made it clear, even to Sky, that pushing for more information would only lead to more shouting and no further clarification. So Sky had left it at that, and let his mind whirl about the possibilities instead.

They needed to get the two Kenyans out of the Underworld before bringing Gayle to Saluverus. That much was clear. But how to find them... The Underworld was made up of seven separate underground empires, each consisting of hundreds of smaller districts, interconnected by a vast network of tunnels. Each territory was directly beneath each of the continents of the earth, but not always matching in size. For example, the European Underworld only covered a third of the European countries. Countries like Spain, the United Kingdom and a lot of south eastern Europe didn't have the Underworld underneath them at all. Scandinavia didn't either.

The different territories in the Underworld might be smaller than the continents above ground, but the areas were still enormous. Even if they knew which King had ordered the kidnapping and torture of the Okoth family, it was still like looking for a needle in a haystack. But at least it would be a smaller haystack.

Sky was itching to do something. *Anything.* His hands clenched and unclenched into fists at his side. His brothers and sister were too tired to either notice or care about the energy rolling through him. He knew how they described him: rash and impulsive. He preferred to think of himself as unpredictable. His methods had never failed him before. Even if they had got them into danger every now and again, it had also brought them great success and victory in the Underworld.

He had just about enough restraint not to shimmer to the African Underworld on the spot. That territory seemed like the best place to start. Disciples didn't have magic of their own. They had affinities for certain skills like Affinites did. Only the Kings had magic, so Sky would bet that even if Reth and Yaro's kidnapping had been ordered by a King whose territory wasn't underneath Africa, the two of them would still be there for now.

So Sky would start tomorrow. And he'd start with Africa's Underworld.

He wouldn't go there immediately; not just yet. He needed to refresh his memory of the African Underworld. He almost laughed out loud at the thought of first going into the library. It was more like him to shimmer from Saluverus there and then. His siblings would laugh at him in amazement for doing some research; he couldn't even remember the last time he'd opened a book.

But this wasn't just any impulsive rescue mission. This mission involved Gayle Mendosa, their future Queen. Even Sky was just about sensible enough to know that, this time, he had to prepare before making a move. The fact that he couldn't even remember the name of the African King said enough about him needing a book before rushing down into that specific Underworld territory.

Sky wouldn't tell his siblings about his plans. They would disapprove, Matu especially. He was always a stickler for rules and protocols and orders. Even if it did involve people Matu was extremely close to. If he got a whiff of Sky's plans he would go straight to Axel to stop him. The Ambassador probably had a plan of his own to get Reth and Yaro out, but Sky already knew that whatever Axel came up with, he would disagree. So, he'd make his own plan. And he'd follow his own plan.

Tomorrow.

He would start tomorrow.

The Asters had spent most of the walk to their rooms in silence. As they stepped into their common room, they absently bade each other goodnight and vanished behind their bedroom doors. Sky remained in the common room for a while. He stared into the fire crackling in the fireplace.

Axel's plan for protecting the other Affinites in the world wasn't unreasonable. It was the Affinites' own responsibility if they chose to remain in their homes and at risk of Disciples breaking in and tearing them away from the Surface. Sky had no doubt that a few paranoid families would be arriving on Saluverus tomorrow, which would make the castle just a little bit busier than usual.

But it was the lack of a plan regarding Reth and Yaro that was nagging at him. Sky moved his head to the side and cracked his neck once, and then did the same to the other side. Then he started his ascent up the stairs to his bedroom. He didn't want to be thinking about the torture currently being inflicted upon Reth to get him to speak, let alone what they were doing to thirteen-year-old Yaro right now.

Sky needed a distraction...

It was a good thing he had one.

Opening his bedroom door awoke the girl lying in his bed. She stretched her arms and brushed some of her long brown hair out of her face as she took him in.

"You're back early," she said.

Sky vaguely remembered the girl telling him her name the evening before, as he pulled off his leather jacket and tugged off the shirt underneath.

So much for getting some sleep, he thought to himself as the girl smiled in anticipation and waited for him to climb into bed.

Chapter 6

It was normal for Sophie to be sitting on one of the large velvet sofas in the Asters' common room, reading a book in the morning. What, to her disgust, had also become normal, was that, while she was sitting there peacefully, Sky's bedroom door would open up above her but he wouldn't be the one to emerge.

This morning wasn't any different.

Sophie had only just settled onto the sofa when the bedroom door opened and a girl stepped out onto the balcony. Her hair was still wet, probably from the shower Sky always *encouraged* the girls to take, and she was wearing the same clothes as she had done the night before. Sophie forced herself to keep her face neutral as the girl – Grace, Sophie believed her name was – red-faced and embarrassed, hurried down the stairs, passed Sophie and left the tower.

Once the door shut behind Grace, Sophie rolled her eyes. Sky had a reputation, and yet *still* girls seemed to throw themselves at him, knowing whatever they had wouldn't last longer than a week at best, a night at worst. Maybe they all thought he could be changed; that the handsome, but emotionally distant and non-committal boy would change *for them*.

Sophie shook her head. They were all clueless. Sophie couldn't remember the last time Sky had taken the time to actually get to know a girl. She doubted whether Sky even knew this girl's name was Grace.

Sophie returned to her book. She had almost rid herself of the image in her head when Sky's bedroom door opened once again and her brother emerged. His blonde hair was wet too, and it was dripping onto the white t-shirt he was wearing. He was holding a black sweatshirt in his hand as he headed down the stairs.

"You're reading early. Had breakfast already?"

Sophie nodded. "Couldn't sleep well."

"Shame." Sky grinned. "I slept great."

Sophie narrowed her eyes at him. "You're disgusting."

"Don't be mean."

"Don't take advantage of every girl on the island and maybe I'll stop."

Sky sniffed and came up behind Sophie. He leaned with his arms on the back of the sofa and looked over her shoulder. "What are you reading?" he asked.

"I doubt it would interest you," Sophie said slyly.

"True. I'm off to get some breakfast. I worked up quite an appetite."

Sophie felt him grinning behind her. She let go of her book with one hand and threw her arm back, elbow first. She caught him right on his cheekbone.

"Ow!" Sky exclaimed, stumbling back slightly.

"*Aster of Speed*, my arse," Sophie chuckled.

"I didn't exactly expect to be attacked in the common room," Sky grumbled. Sophie looked over her shoulder and found Sky rubbing his cheek with his hands. There was a sparkle of amusement in his eyes.

"If you keep saying things like that, you should expect it," Sophie told him.

Sky laughed and shook his head. "Later, sis." He leaned in and kissed her on the cheek.

Sophie batted his head away. "Don't kiss me with that mouth!"

Laughing, Sky headed for the door. "It's clean! I just showered."

"Yeah, with her!" Sophie called after him. Still laughing, he turned in the open doorway, and only just ducked in time to avoid the cushion Sophie had thrown at his head. When he straightened up, he winked at her and closed the door behind him.

Sophie sighed and stared out in front of her. In moments like these she was very glad that they all had their own bedrooms. And their own bathrooms. Sophie would've felt extreme pity for whoever would have to share with Sky in another life where they didn't have that luxury.

An hour passed and Sophie had barely got through ten pages. She checked her watch. Her mind kept wandering to the Board Room. She wondered who from the Small Council was there now, checking the signals that would be starting to come in right about now. It was nine o'clock in the morning on Saluverus, which would mean – Sophie closed her eyes and calculated – that it would be ten o'clock in the evening in Hawaii right now.

There were three families in Hawaii that Sophie knew of. None of them were much in contact with the Small Council. The head of the Kahale family would send word to Nicholas every now and again, though their training programme was nothing compared to Reth Okath's Academy in Kenya. The Hawaiian families basically just trained their own children, and there were group sessions every now and again where the children of one family would learn new skills from other parents.

Not all Affinites were soldiers. It depended on their affinity where they would be stationed during a war, but all Affinites were trained to a standard minimum, and were more than capable of training their children to know, and be capable of, the same.

Sophie breathed slowly as she kept looking at her watch. It would be in the ten minutes after each hour that the Asters could be called in. Axel had sent out the new protocols for all Affinite families on the Surface that morning, and Hawaii was the first country with Affinites to hit the next hour mark.

Ten past, and no call; Sophie loosed a breath of relief.

"Waiting to be summoned?" a voice asked behind her.

Sophie turned her head to find Nathan standing in the doorway of his bedroom, which was on the same floor as the common room. She sighed and stared at the ceiling.

"I don't want to be," she admitted.

"Don't want to be waiting or don't want to be summoned?" Nathan asked, moving around to the front of the sofa. Sophie pulled in her legs so Nathan could sit down next to her. Instinctively she placed her legs on his lap. He looked down at them for a second.

"Both. It's stupid."

Nathan placed a hand on Sophie's knee. His wavy brown hair was still wet from his shower. He wasn't looking at her; his eyes were on the hand that was on her knee. "It's not stupid."

"It's just... what they did to Eidi..."

"You saved her life, Sophie." The kindness in his voice made her heart contract. Nathan was always kind. Whether he meant to be or not. Sophie remembered the coldness in his voice when he spoke about Reth and Yaro not being killed *yet*, in the Board Room the night before. He had seemed so detached then. He was always like that; as if there was this separating line between being an Aster and just being a person; being cold and clinical and being kind and quiet.

"I still shouldn't get emotional," Sophie said. Nathan finally looked up at her, and pulled a face as if she was being ridiculous.

"I am a warrior," Sophie said with an exaggerated voice, which made Nathan chuckle. "I am not supposed to have feelings."

"You weren't emotional when you were holding her intestines in your hands while she was still alive and un-sedated. You were a warrior then. You're allowed to have feelings now." He didn't speak loudly. When he was off duty, Nathan never spoke loudly. He didn't have Sky's outward swagger, Matu's radiating strength or Lian's relaxed, cheerful nature. He had that quiet calm and thoughtful silence that had the ability to ground you.

Sophie smiled gratefully and reached over to hold Nathan's hand in hers. Nathan's eyes flickered to her hand for a second before looking up at her again. "Thanks... But we're not really off duty now, are we?"

Nathan used the hand he was holding to pull Sophie's arm closer towards him. Sophie opened her mouth to ask what he was doing, but she realised soon enough. He was looking at the watch on her wrist. "We're off duty for the next fifty minutes," he said thoughtfully. "We should do something other than dread what could happen in fifty minutes."

"Or thirty," Sophie pointed out. "Some countries are another half an hour ahead of others. Some only fifteen minutes."

Nathan gave her a look. "Only you would know that. Just try not to think about it too much, okay? We'll be summoned when we're summoned."

Sophie bit her lip. "Sorry."

Nathan chuckled slightly. "However, *until* then..."

Before Sophie could say anything, Nathan pushed her legs off his lap and stood up. He extended a hand to Sophie and pulled her off the sofa as well.

"Where are we going?" she asked.

"You're not allowed to know yet," Nathan said. The right-hand corner of his lips twitched up momentarily. Nathan shrugged on his jacket and was about to lead them out of the common room when he seemed to remember something. He walked over to the small fridge near his bedroom door and pulled it open. For people who didn't know much about the Asters, they would've been shocked to find that the fridge was not filled with food, but with vials of blood.

Each vial had a sticker on the side that depicted one of the Asters' symbols, indicating whose blood it contained.

Nathan grabbed one of the vials with Sky's wing on the sticker and put it safely in an inside pocket of his jacket. He looked over to Sophie who was quietly watching what he was doing. Nathan shrugged his shoulders. "For when they summon us at short notice."

Sophie wondered where he would be taking her. Apparently far enough that they wouldn't be able to get to the Board Room within a few minutes. Asters could harness each other's magic for a single moment through each other's blood. By drinking only a drop of Sky's blood, a Band just like Sky's would appear on the other Aster's wrist, right beside their own, and that Aster would be able to harness Sky's magic of either speed, flight or shimmering that single time. By taking some of Sky's blood with them, Sophie and Nathan could go wherever they wanted on the island, and be in the Board Room within seconds of being summoned.

When the Asters had just started training together, years ago, learning how to harness Sophie's magic had been one of the first things the boys had been taught. Since her magic allowed Sophie to heal only others but not herself, this was a perfect failsafe to still get healed if she herself sustained a life-threatening injury.

Sophie smiled at Nathan's thinking of bringing some of Sky's blood, and followed him out of the common room, excited to discover whatever Nathan had thought of to keep their minds off the possible mission that they could be summoned for at any time.

Much to Sky's surprise Lian was having breakfast in the dining hall when he walked in. He would have expected all his brothers to still be sleeping at eight o'clock in the morning.

Sky nodded to his brother and then made his way to stand in line at the buffet. It was a little busier than usual for this time of day. Affinite orphans were all having breakfast before going off to school in the town. Any Affinite who had lost their parents before they reached the age of eighteen was brought to live in the castle's orphan-wing, and were looked after by care-givers, who also lived in the castle.

Sky had got used to the number of orphans that lived in the castle. In the war fought by his mother and the other Asters of the previous generation – called Ceders – many children had lost their parents. When Sky was very young, there had been more orphans living in the castle than there had ever been before or since. Though those war-orphans were over eighteen now and had moved out, others had come in their places. They ranged from all ages, though the majority of them were between twelve and seventeen years old.

Once an orphan turned eighteen, they were allowed to go back and live in their parents' home if they wanted to, and if such a home still existed. Otherwise they were allowed to remain in the castle for as long as it took them to get a job and get a place for themselves.

Sky walked over to one of the four long tables with his breakfast and sat down across from his brother. Lian was deep in conversation with Anna, who was sitting next to him. Anna was a seventeen-year-old English Affinite with an affinity for health. From one of his conversations with her, Sky remembered she was going to study to become a doctor at the Medical Bay of Saluverus. Lian and Anna had become close friends this past year.

The Asters were always allowed to go home and visit their parents on weekends and holidays if they weren't on active duty, or actively waiting for a mission to happen. A year earlier Lian had lost his parents in a house fire and suddenly had no family to go home to when weekends and holidays came around. So he remained on Saluverus when the other

Asters went to their respective families. It was during one of those times that Lian had met Anna.

"So where will you go when you turn eighteen?" Lian was asking her.

"I'll probably stay here for a while longer. I have to start my nurse training before even thinking about becoming a doctor, and that won't leave much space for me to earn money and have my own place just yet," Anna answered.

"That sounds all right. You know you can stay here for as long as you need," Lian said.

Sky barely looked up from his breakfast as the two of them talked.

"Yes, I know. And even though most of my friends live in the town, there are just about enough nice people around here to keep me company." She winked at Lian.

Lian grinned at her. "Well, I'm glad you think so."

Date her already, Sky thought as he rolled his eyes to his cereal. Though he knew not to talk about that particular subject with Lian anymore. Even though his parents had died, Lian still loyally clung on to their plans to marry him off to some Affinite he had never met before. All down the Fai bloodline the tradition of arranged marriage had been followed, where their bride or groom had been chosen for them. Lian knew his parents had already chosen a bride for him, and he wasn't about to spoil their memory by breaking with his family's tradition.

Anna knew this and had stayed his friend for the past twelve months, even though Sky could see from the way that she looked at his brother that she wouldn't mind having more. Yet she had never pushed it, and Sky, despite, or perhaps because of, his own shenanigans, respected her very much for it.

The two friends across from him continued to talk and laugh their way all through Sky's breakfast. He was glad to be finished so that he didn't have to listen any more. He knew that if he just got up and left Lian wouldn't even have noticed, so to make sure that Lian knew where

Sky was in case they needed to get to the Board Room quickly he said, "I'll be in the library if you need to find me."

Lian looked up at that, surprised. "What the hell are you going to be doing in a library?"

His surprise was justified. Sky hadn't set foot in the library for months. He felt that his energy was better spent in the arena, since Sophie knew everything they ever needed to know, anyway. It always made more sense to him to prepare for battle, not for a quiz show.

"Don't," Sky warned.

"Are you sure you still know where it is?" Lian joked. Beside him, Anna chuckled.

"Shut up," Sky snapped. He couldn't stop grinning however, as he turned around and walked away.

"You sure I don't need to draw you a map?" Lian called after him.

"I can't hear you!" Sky called over his shoulder, though of course he could hear the two of them laughing as he left the dining hall and headed up the west-wing stairs to the library.

Hours passed and still no summoning. That morning, before heading for the stables in the town, Nathan and Sophie had grabbed a few sandwiches from the dining hall breakfast buffet. They had run into Lian there, and their brother had promised to join them a while later after Anna had gone to her classes.

Nathan had taken Sophie down to the stables where they borrowed two horses. They had ridden them all the way up to the pine forest at the north end of the island. For hours the two of them rode through the woods, rarely having to double back on themselves because of its size. They paused every time it was ten o'clock somewhere else in the world to see whether an Affinite family didn't send their signal in on time.

No summoning ever came, which meant that until now every Affinite family in the world was accounted for.

Sophie did most of the talking as they rode, and Nathan spent the time listening to her going on and on about some myth or legend she had read about. Sophie loved old stories of long lost worlds and ancient peoples. It didn't interest Nathan much, but he loved watching Sophie's eyes light up as she talked about it. How she could find practically everything interesting Nathan would never understand. He wondered if it was part of her magic of Knowledge, or if it was just something personal to Sophie.

At the end of the day Nathan would probably have forgotten most of what Sophie had been talking about. The death rituals of the ancient Egyptians were something Nathan didn't particularly want to remember. His ears, however, pricked up when she started talking about myths that involved Queen Aiyana. It was interesting hearing stories about their first ever Queen; how it was said she had a sword that could cut through anything, and a shield that protected her against everything, including the magic of Lightning, a magic that the Dark King, Astaroth, always sent with the wave of his signature double–bladed axe. Legend said those two weapons possessed the same magic Aiyana did, but there was no evidence to suggest this was true. To both Sophie and Nathan's knowledge, those two weapons had never existed. If they did, they would surely know about it.

Lian and Matu had joined them around three in the afternoon. The two of them had practised their archery that morning. The two boys had also arrived on horseback. That and cycling were the most common ways to move around on the island.

The four of them had ridden to the edge of the forest and onto a small clearing at the northern-most tip of the island. They had tied their horses to nearby trees and sat down on the edge, their feet dangling off the cliff face as they stared out onto the darkening Norwegian Sea.

Sophie had asked why Sky hadn't joined them, only to hear the most surprising news of all: Sky had been in the library all day and hadn't wanted to leave. It had left her struggling for air as the four of them imagined Sky behind a pile of books, researching God knows what.

When the sun set at around five o'clock the four Asters built a fire and ate their simple packed snacks in silence. They used to come here all the time when they were children. Nathan knew Sophie needed a day like today. When they were on duty and out in the world on missions Sophie was fierce and brutal, while somehow able to be witty and sharp whenever any of the boys stepped out of line. Sky was usually the recipient of this, just like he had been when he had mistakenly pronounced Eidi as dead. When they weren't on duty Sophie was still witty and sharp, but also softer, kinder.

"Eleven past five," Sophie said, looking at her watch. "All Affinites in parts of Bangladesh, Bhutan, China and Russia accounted for."

"Good," Lian breathed.

"That's nearly half the world down," Matu said.

"For now," Sophie whispered.

Nathan offered her a smile. "Small victories," he told her.

Sophie looked at him and covered her hand with his. Nathan's eyes flickered to her hand for a moment before turning back to look out onto the sea, his smile lingering on his face.

When the fire burned down the four Asters finally packed up their things, got back on their horses, and headed back to the stables. They made the descent down through the forest in almost complete darkness. They had come here so often that none of them were afraid they'd get lost in the forest. And the horses probably knew the way back from memory, as well.

After they cleaned, fed and locked the horses in their stables for the night the four of them headed back to the castle for a late dinner before heading for bed. Nathan hoped he would fall asleep quickly. He, as they all did, knew that they needed to get as much sleep as they could, since their night could be cut short, just like it had been the evening before.

Nathan prayed that the rest of the world would be left alone. And he also prayed that Gayle Mendosa, wherever she was, was all right, too. He hoped for her sake that she enjoyed these last few blissful weeks. Because little did she know that her world would be thrown upside down in less than a month. And there would be no going back.

Chapter 7

Sky hadn't expected to still be in the damn library the afternoon of the following day. For a few minutes every hour he would stop what he was doing and stare at his watch. His heart would race every time the clock struck the hour, and he would stay still, staring at the moving hand for every one of the next ten minutes that went by.

It was five past two. Signals would be coming in in floods right about now. Sky didn't exactly know where from. From the geography book he had laid open during his research he assumed they had made it to eastern Australia. But he could be wrong. He never looked at a map any longer than he needed to; only to know where to shimmer to. So how would he possibly know which time zones were where? He still didn't understand why England was one hour behind them while on the map it looked like it was right above France and Spain, but those two countries had the same time as Saluverus and the rest of Europe.

The minute hand on his watch moved to eleven past two and Sky sighed in relief. He leaned back against one of the hundreds of bookshelves of the library and closed his eyes. The library was an immense space. It covered three stories, and every single wall was covered in bookshelves; the higher ones could be reached by spiral staircases and narrow balconies. On the bottom floor tables and chairs were scattered in between the many extra bookcases that had been set up over the years. There were small lamps on each of the tables. They were necessary, as the dark wood of the bookcases and the millions of books caused the library to have a dark, gloomy feel. Light came in through the windows high above the top bookcases on the third level, but the weather was horrible today; rain was lashing against the windows and the cloudy sky made the library even darker.

Sky kept his eyes closed for a moment longer. How long would they have to wait with dread until the unknown King and his Disciples made their next move? He hated looking at his watch every five minutes, expecting every minute that the hour had come around again. It didn't help him in his research.

He didn't know his way around the library the way that Sophie did. He could ask one of the librarians for help, but he didn't want news getting out that he was researching everything that had to do with the African Underworld. He wanted information on which King was in control of it, he wanted to know the names and faces of that King's inner circle, and he wanted a map.

There were Mergers – Affinite spies who integrated into undercover life in the Underworld – all over the place, picking up information and drawing maps and sending whatever else they could find out back to the Small Council through Felix. Sky knew there were recent maps of the African Underworld somewhere. He knew that it didn't matter that everyone on the island could get their hands on them. Affinites couldn't get into the Underworld even if they wanted to. There were entrances, but their precise location could not be found in any of the books here. A few Watchers who lived close to an entrance knew the location of that single one, because it was important for the Small Council to know as much about the comings and goings of Disciples as possible. Sky knew where some entrances were, but he doubted Reth and Yaro would be kept anywhere near those. Once Sky had narrowed down where the two Affinites were being kept, he would have to magically create another entrance, so he would have to deal with as little Disciple resistance as possible.

Luckily for him, he already knew how to do that.

He would take some of Nathan's blood and channel his brother's magic to create a door in the ground. Nathan did it every time they had to venture into the Underworld. Back in the Original War, Queen Aiyana and the first Aster of Flora had created the Underworld and banished the Kings and Disciples there. Since the Kings were immortal, Aiyana chose to create a place for them to exist, but where they could do no harm to the humans living above. The Kings and Disciples were able to return to the Surface; there was nothing Aiyana could do to trap them there forever, but with the army she had raised, the Kings were better off staying underground. There had been a few uprisings throughout history, but no King had ever succeeded in taking back the Surface.

Sky realised he'd been standing with his back against the bookcase, with his eyes closed, for quite a while when suddenly a voice snapped him back to reality.

"*Sky Mayne?*" There was mockery in the boy's voice. Sky didn't need to open his eyes to know who it was.

"Walk away, Jacob."

"It *is* you." Jacob made an exaggerated gasp. "This is one for the history books. Sky bloody Mayne is in a library."

Slowly, Sky opened his eyes and turned his head to the left.

Jacob Henderson stood at the end of the bookcase, his arms crossed over his chest and a very amused grin on his face. His sandy blonde hair had grown longer than usual, and now reached the top of his eyes. Jacob brushed the hair away from his forehead, his brown eyes twinkling as he looked at Sky.

"You really don't want to do this with me right now," Sky warned.

"What's the matter, Aussie? Got dizzy walking around in circles trying to find the right book?" Jacob joked. "Do you want me to get a nurse?"

Sky smirked. "Yes, get me a nurse. Preferable around the age of twenty."

Jacob chuckled humourlessly. "You haven't changed."

"Yeah, neither have you," Sky retorted, contemptuously.

Jacob cocked his head to the side and narrowed his eyes. "So why is the *legendary* Sky Mayne in a library? Finally figured out the next mission will kill you if you don't open a book once in a while?"

"In your dreams am I ever going to die," Sky snarled.

Jacob grinned coldly. "Ah, right."

Both of them knew Sky wasn't far off the point. Jacob did dream of him dying. It sounded harsh, but it was true. Jacob dreamed of becoming an Aster. He trained for it every day of his life. Yes, Asters were born through blood; a parent needed to be one for the child to inherit the magic. But an Affinite could become one should the worst happen. For as long as an Aster didn't have a child yet on whom to pass on his or her magic, and that Aster was to die, the magic could be extracted from the body and passed on to an Affinite. That Affinite would then become an Aster, and his or her child would be one, too. That way the Aster magic would never die out.

Jacob was half moving away when he turned his head back towards Sky. "How's Sophie doing these days? Looking forward to the Queen arriving soon, right? She must be very excited."

"You stay away from my sister," Sky snapped. He couldn't stomach the idea of Jacob going anywhere near Sophie.

"But she isn't *really* your sister, is she, though?" Jacob said, amused. He knew he always hit a nerve when he brought up Sophie in the conversation.

Sky narrowed his eyes at the English boy with an affinity for strategy. "She is in every way that counts. And if you even attempt to hurt her, I will risk being thrown into the Frozen Dungeons to rip out your throat."

"Oooh." Jacob held his hands in the air in mocking surrender. "And we all know how ruthless you can be. Or is it flying around like a little fairy, with your sparkly blue lights, that makes you particularly intimidating?"

"Pretty words for a boy with no magic," Sky taunted.

"I don't need any the way you always seem to."

"For ripping your throat out, neither do I."

Jacob saw the blazing in Sky's eyes and knew he had done enough to rile him. Sky wasn't just known to be impulsive and rash amongst his brothers and sister. Though he had never lost his temper amongst Affinites, Jacob could imagine that if it were ever to happen, he would be the recipient of it.

Instead of seeming nervous, Jacob laughed instead. Sky narrowed his eyes at him. Jacob waved his hand and turned around to walk away. "Happy reading, *Aster*. Maybe you'll finally figure out how to spell your own name."

Sky growled at Jacob's back. He shook himself mentally and forced himself to calm down. It was no use getting all worked up over Jacob Henderson. All that boy lived for was to get under their skin, and to learn and train hard enough that if one of them died, he might gain one of the Asters' magic for himself. Sky would fight until his last breath to make sure *that* would never happen.

Sky shook his head once again and returned to the little round table he had made his own. Two piles of books were stacked on top of it, and a single book lay open on a page with the world map and its time zones. Sky sat down and stared at the world map. A part of Asia and the West Coast of Australia would be next to call in.

He turned his attention to the pile of books on the right and pulled off the top one. He had looked in this one before. It was filled with maps of the Underworld. Each page depicted layouts of the various districts of each of the territories. Some were extremely detailed. As Sky flipped through the pages in search of a specific map he had already found earlier that day, his gaze momentarily rested on the floor plan of the throne room, and a few of the surrounding rooms, in the underground castle of the capital district of the North American Underworld.

Sky kept the page open for a while and examined the rooms. The detail in the map was incredible. That a Merger would have to have been up close in all these rooms, and for long periods of time, to sketch them out at this level of perfection – and get them back out to the Surface undetected – was hard for Sky to fathom.

He looked at the bottom of the map and saw a name scribbled at the bottom. *A. Jones*, it said. Sky didn't do much research. Or any real research for that matter. But even he knew who Agatha Jones was. She was her own kind of special. She was an Indigo: an Affinite born with not just one affinity inherited from one parent, but with both affinities from each parent. The amalgamation of the two affinities led to a crackle of raw energy that bordered on magical. She couldn't cast spells or perform magic in the way that the Asters could. But her affinity had been magnified to such an extent that she could not be considered just another Affinite. Indigos came along as often as a scientific genius did; once, possibly twice in a generation, if the world was lucky enough.

Sky had always wanted to meet her, but the woman had been in the Underworld ever since Sky had known her name. She never re-surfaced. She was like a ghost. Some Affinites even went as far as to claim that Agatha Jones never existed at all.

Sky smirked at the idea as he continued his way through the book. After the section on the North American Underworld came the South American Underworld. These maps were quite dated. No new information about the layout of that territory had come through in the last twenty-five years. Even before King Astaroth's death, it had always been impossible for Mergers to get into the capital district of the South American Underworld without blowing their cover. But since the King's death, parts of the capital had been closed off completely from Disciples, too; only the highest ranking Disciples had access to those parts.

Astaroth had been the most powerful King the world had ever known, and he had also been one of the original seven. He had been killed in the war twenty-five years ago by the Ceders, the previous generation of Asters, but no one knew how they'd managed to do it. It was said Tomas Mendosa, Gayle Mendosa's father, had been the one to deliver the killer blow, but something had happened in the aftermath of that duel that had messed with his memory. Some last gasp effect of Astaroth's magic of Lightning, perhaps. Sky remembered his mother telling him how she had found Tomas standing over Astaroth's body, but him having no idea how it had happened.

Sky grazed his hand over the double-bladed axe drawn on the bottom right corner of the page; Astaroth's signature weapon and that of his inner circle and other highly ranked soldiers. Every Aster and Affinite in the world would recognise the weapon anywhere. If the Asters were ever to encounter that axe, with the red gemstone in the middle and the thin red carvings that decorated the blades, they knew they were in big trouble. Astaroth had been the most powerful King in history. His successor wouldn't be weaker. And the worst part was that, until this day, no one knew who his successor was.

Sky shook himself mentally. There was no point worrying about an unknown King in South America, when he had a very real and very well-known King to deal with in Africa.

Sky gave the double-bladed axe one more glance before turning the pages until he reached the part in the book that focused on the African Underworld, ruled by the one hundred and twenty-seven-year-old King Brys.

Earlier that day, Sky had marked a few pages and for the last time he would attempt to memorise the route he would take that evening. He had narrowed down the places where Yaro and Reth could be held to two spots, and they weren't as far away from each other as Sky had feared.

For another half an hour he went over the plan in his head. He knew exactly where on the Surface of the earth he would shimmer to, after which he would take Nathan's blood to use his magic of Flora to open up the earth and form an entrance leading down into the Underworld. Sky drilled the map into his brain; he forced himself to remember every door, every corner and every corridor. He knew where he'd have to turn left twice and he knew where he was most likely to encounter the first Disciples, were they to detect his presence.

Again and again he replayed his plan in his head. His brothers and sister would understand why he had left. They would understand why he hadn't told them. He would leave a note. They would know where he was and how to find him if he was gone for longer than two days without sending a signal for his well-being.

They would be angry when they found out he had vanished.

"*Are you out of your mind?*" came a voice from behind him.

Or they would be angry now, Sky thought. He closed his eyes and turned around slowly. When he opened his eyes again Sophie was standing over him, her hands on her hips, staring at the map of the African Underworld lying before him.

"What the hell do you think you're doing?"

Sky bit his lip. "Wouldn't you already know? Since you're the smart one?"

It was the wrong thing to say, because before he knew it, he was clutching his cheek where she had slapped him across his face.

"Don't you dare take that tone," Sophie snapped. Her thunderstorm grey eyes were blazing in anger. "You are planning to go to the African Underworld *by yourself*? Are you really that stupid?"

Sky shoved his chair back and stood up. Being nearly a head taller than her, he towered over her. But that didn't intimidate her. Sophie lifted her chin and glared angrily at her brother.

"I can't just sit here and do nothing! You know that!"

"So you decide to go on a suicide mission?"

"It's not a—"

But Sky got interrupted by the head librarian, popping her head around the nearest bookcase and shushing them. Both Sky and Sophie muttered their apologies and waited for the librarian to move on before turning back to glare at each other again.

"It's not a suicide mission!" Sky whispered angrily. "I've done my research."

"Oh, research my arse. You don't even know if they're in Africa!" Sophie hissed.

"Odds are they are."

"You know what are greater odds? That you get killed trying to find two people who won't even be where you will be looking."

"And where should I be looking?" Sky paused for a moment. "You know something."

"Of course I know something. I know everything!"

"Then tell me!"

"I'm not telling you anything."

"Why not?"

"Because I'm coming with you."

That made Sky pause. Sophie never agreed with his impulsive decision-making, let alone joined him into carrying out whatever plan he had concocted.

"You *what?* Why?"

"Because you're going to go no matter what I say."

"What does that have to do with you going?"

"Because you need my brains to keep you alive." Sophie moved around Sky and picked up the book with the map of the African Underworld. Sky had drawn two red circles around the places where he had decided the best chances were to find Reth and Yaro. Sophie held the book up and pointed at one of the two circles. "There is no way they will be here."

"Why not?"

"Because this map is ten years old and those rows of dungeons collapsed during an earthquake two years ago, you dumbass."

"How is it possible that you know that?" Sky exclaimed.

Another shushing came from further down in the library. Sky looked round briefly at where the sound came from, before looking back at Sophie's livid face.

"Because I do more research than opening a single book in two years and think I know everything about an entire Underworld territory!" Sophie hissed. "If you went there now, you'd not only come face to face with a collapsed dungeon. You wouldn't be anywhere near Reth and Yaro. And you would've been detected."

"So what if I'm detected? I can shimmer out just fine. Why do you think I didn't ask anyone to come with me? If we got separated then we'd be screwed."

"*That's* your reasoning?" Sophie raised her eyebrows at him as if he was completely missing her point. "Then let me ask you this. If the African King isn't behind this, you really want him to retaliate for breaking into his territory while we're already dealing with another King? You really want to be the reason we have to fight off not one, but two Kings at the same time?"

"If you really believe all that, then why are you putting so little effort into talking me out of it? Why immediately say you're coming with me?"

Sophie crossed her arms. "Because I know you. And you will still go because you *don't think.*"

Sky narrowed his eyes at her. "You don't agree with me just a little?"

Sophie sniffed. "I'm not a fan of waiting around while the next Affinite gets taken. *But—*" she added the second Sky opened his mouth to agree, "that doesn't mean I'm condoning this plan in the slightest, you understand me? You realise this would've killed you."

"I would've found a way out. You know I would've."

"Don't push it," Sophie warned.

Sky nodded. "All right, fine! Let's go get the others, then."

He was about to pass her to walk out of the library when she caught his arm and pulled him back to stand in front of her. "Woah, woah, woah, where do you think you're going?"

"On a secret mission," Sky threw back at her, "that will probably get us both killed *and* could start a war with a King who has nothing to do with this, right? So I'm getting our brothers. *You* wanted to come. Why wouldn't they?"

"You are not dragging anyone else into this!"

Sky stared at her. "You dragged yourself into this!"

"That is not the point."

"Come *on*. Nathan would come."

"*Do not* drag Nathan into this."

"He can make a door! And possibly an escape route if necessary."

Sophie shook her head vigorously. "No. Not a chance. He should not be a part of this."

"He's so protective of all of us. Especially of you. If we tell him, he'll come along without us actually asking," Sky reasoned

"*Precisely.* He will come along *for us*, even if he doesn't believe it's the right thing."

"You don't believe it's the right thing either," Sky reminded her.

"What did I tell you about pushing it?" Sophie exhaled heavily. "I should just have you thrown in the castle dungeons."

"Then why don't you?"

Sophie gave Sky a look. "Because you know a way out."

Sky relaxed his shoulders and gave a very self-satisfied grin. "I do... Ow!"

Sophie had slapped him on the shoulder this time.

Another *shush* came from somewhere in the library.

Sky glared at Sophie, but her eyes said everything: she had made up her mind and there was no changing it.

"Fine. Not Nathan. What about Lian? He'd join in a heartbeat to save them," Sky said.

Sophie thought about this for a moment. Sky couldn't think why she would have to think so hard. They had both heard the edge in Lian's voice back in the Board Room. Ever since his parents had died in that house fire Lian could not stand an order of backing down when someone was out there suffering. Lian wouldn't be hard to convince to come along, even if it was a suicide mission. It would be his own choice, whereas Nathan would have to overcome his own conscience to help them.

Then Sophie nodded slowly, once. "Lian would want to. Matu wouldn't, though."

"Of course Matu wouldn't. I wasn't going to try him," Sky said quickly. Matu would be the last person they should tell about their secret plan to storm the African Underworld.

"Well, you did say you wanted the "others"," Sophie pointed out.

"I didn't mean Matu!"

"Who didn't mean Matu?"

Sky and Sophie seemed to freeze at the same time. They had spent so much time hissing at each other that they hadn't noticed Matu come up in between the rows of bookcases.

"What are you guys doing?" Matu asked, as he approached the table Sky had been working at. Neither Sky nor Sophie said anything as Matu took one look at the books on the table and immediately looked up at them furiously. *"Are you out of your mind?"*

"You sound just like Sophie," Sky replied, attempting to deflect Matu's anger.

Sophie narrowed her eyes at Sky and pushed the book she had been holding into his chest. "It was his idea."

Sky glared at Sophie, but it was obvious she hadn't expected Matu to appear any more than he had. What Matu had been doing in the library was anybody's guess.

"But you were going to go with him?" Matu said accusingly to Sophie.

Sophie placed her hands on her hips again. Matu was even taller than Sky was, and a lot wider, with all that muscle on his arms and chest. It made no difference to Sophie. Nothing any of the boys did ever intimidated her. She always held her own without any problem.

"I didn't want him to get killed," Sophie snapped.

"That's no excuse. You're defying direct orders!"

Another, louder *shush* came from behind the shelves.

"You could come with us," Sky offered. Sophie rolled her eyes and threw her hands up in exasperation.

"Excuse me?" Matu asked, with deceptive calm.

"We want to find Reth and Yaro *before* the Disciples find out Reth doesn't know Gayle Mendosa's location. We know you do, too. You know they'll kill both of them once they find out." Sky knew it was a cheap shot but it was the only card he could play. Reth was like a second father to Matu. If there was anything that could lead Matu to break the rules, then this would be it.

Fury was written all over Matu's features. "You know I want to save them as much as you do. *More even*. But that doesn't mean we go off by ourselves on a whim to see if we magically stumble upon them when we have *no idea* where they are! We don't even know if they're in Africa!"

"Of course they're in Africa! What King is powerful and daring enough to attack on another King's continent?" Sky countered.

Matu threw his hands up in the air and muttered something in Swahili. He always turned to his native Kenyan language when he had trouble controlling his emotions, usually when he was frustrated or angry. Lian did the same in Japanese in similar situations.

When Matu finished his short string of Swahili words he narrowed his eyes to Sky and said slowly, as if talking to a dimwit, "Axel has a plan for a reason."

"Oh come on! Waiting for another family to get attacked and hoping we're not too late this time, is not a plan!" Sky exclaimed.

"The Small Council gives us orders, and we follow," Matu growled.

"You've *got* to be kidding me. You know you're such a—" But whatever Sky was going to say was cut short. Because at that moment the chip in his upper right arm started twitching frantically. In his surprise Sky stumbled a step backwards. The chip had never twitched like that before and Sky knew that something was very, very wrong. He looked at Matu and Sophie and he guessed he had the same expression on his face as they did.

Sky pointed a finger at Matu. "Not *a word* about this to Axel," he warned.

Matu only glared at Sky more.

Sky threw the book he was holding down onto the table and reached forward and grabbed one of their hands. Knowing someone else would now have to clean up his mess of books in the library, Sky shimmered the three of them to the Board Room, dreading what news the Small Council would have for him and his fellow Asters.

Chapter 8

When Nathan dashed into the Board Room, only Lian wasn't there yet. Sophie, Sky and Matu were standing near the oak table and the members of the Small Council were dispersed around the room. Nathan noticed Matu and Sky glaring at each other with angry expressions on their faces, and there was tension in their stances. Nathan caught Sophie's eye and looked at her questioningly, but she just shook her head.

Less than half a minute passed before blue light appeared and Lian shimmered in. None of them knew where Lian had been moments before, but it must've been far enough away that he thought channelling Sky's magic would be necessary to get to the Board Room in time.

Nicholas Nelson was in the desk chair again and was typing furiously on the keyboard behind the computer. Felix Hauser was leaning over the Emissary's shoulder. The Spymaster had a phone to his ear and was whispering softly to Nicholas as he waited for whoever was on the other end of the line to pick up the phone.

Nathan paid little attention to the Spymaster and Emissary. He and the other Asters went straight for the weapons and other mission-ready kit lying on the round oak table in the middle of the room. As they hurriedly strapped and slipped their various weapons to their belts and into their sheaths, and stowed vials of each other's blood in various pockets, Axel told them what was going on.

"We're going through all the signals as we speak. No word yet from the Brown family down in Perth. Felix can't get into contact with either of the Watchers he'd sent to keep an eye on the house. Hauser—" Axel turned to the Spymaster, who lifted his head from the computer screen, "—any luck with Soto or Benanti?"

"Soto and Benanti were watching the house?" Sophie asked while she strapped the miniature crossbow to her left wrist. Axel didn't answer her. It didn't surprise Nathan that Sophie would recognise the names of Felix's Watchers. She no doubt also knew the spies' skills, and the surprise in her voice told him enough about the wrongness of the situation.

"This is where you need to be," Axel said. He pointed the remote control at the television hanging above the corner desk. A map appeared on the screen, and started zooming in to Australia, then to the west coast, closing in on Perth, and then a specific street. Sky was watching the screen intently. "Keep your phones open for if we need to contact you. The Brown family might not be the only ones in need in this time zone. Go *now*."

All five Asters came together on one side of the table and held each other's hands. Blue light filled Nathan's vision and for a split second he felt the ground under his feet disappear. When there was ground under his feet again, it wasn't the wood of the Board Room; it was asphalt.

The blue light vanished from Nathan's eyes and they found themselves on a dark street. In front of them was a large townhouse, with three floors, two balconies, great windows from floors to ceilings and a large garden and fence spanning around the property. The fact that the gate was hanging off its hinges wasn't a good sign.

Nathan felt the cold calm come over him as the five of them hurried across the street and through the gate. Night had already fallen and it was only thanks to the bright street lighting that Nathan saw anything in the cloudy night. He pulled out the pocket torch from his belt and almost crashed into Matu's back, not realizing that his brother had stopped still, right in front of him.

Nathan stepped around Matu to see why he had stopped.

Sophie was already on her knees, her fingers on the throat of the body lying in front of her.

"Dead," Sophie said matter-of-factly. "Body's still very warm. This can't have happened more than an hour ago."

They'd barely missed the person responsible.

Nathan saw Lian drop his head in disappointment. Nathan didn't feel the same. He didn't feel much when they were on missions. They had their orders. They were to find out what had happened, and if anyone had survived. They were not meant to have feelings right now. Nathan didn't need to look at Sky, for instance, to know that his brother would not be able to hide his fury at being too late, again.

Sophie turned the body onto its side so she could see the face. It was a woman, with short black hair tied into a tiny ponytail, and light skin. Her face was bruised and bloody. Nathan recognised the clothing; this woman was an Affinite. As Sophie turned the woman around completely, Nathan noticed the blood stain just underneath her ribs. That stab wound had been her death.

Nathan didn't recognise the woman. He knew the Brown family, had seen Logan, Orla and their son Eli on special gatherings on Saluverus before. This woman wasn't Orla Brown.

"Fiorella Soto," Sophie announced. She dropped the woman's shoulder and got up. "Let's go."

There was nothing more that they could do for the dead Watcher. Sky hung back for a moment before following the other Asters towards the house. Nathan looked over his shoulder and caught the few blue sparks that remained of a shimmer. Sky had used his magic to shimmer the body to the morgue in the castle back on Saluverus. Only once they had a moment to spare would Axel be informed of what had happened and that the body was where it needed to be for an autopsy.

When Sky had caught up with them, Nathan looked over to Sophie. "Who was she?"

As they pushed through the door and into the dark and silent house, Sophie answered, "Peruvian Affinite. Been working with the Italian Lorenzo Benanti as a Watcher duo for the past year. Their work was flawless." *Until now.* The unspoken words hung heavily in the air.

Matu tried the light switches near the door. The hallway remained dark.

"What a surprise," Sky muttered sarcastically.

Matu ignored him. "Lian, Sophie, you take the bottom floor," he commanded. Lian and Sophie nodded and headed down the hallway, the lights from their torches bouncing off the walls. "Sky take the top floor; Nate and I have the middle."

There was a blue flash, flooding the darkened hallway in light momentarily, and Sky had shimmered. Nathan followed Matu up the winding staircase to the middle floor. He had expected to find a hallway with doors leading to separate bedrooms, but instead the staircase led to a completely open space. If Nathan had visited before the place had been ransacked, a large dining room table would have been standing directly opposite him. That same table, however, was now tipped onto its side. Behind the table against the wall stood a large bookcase. The dark oak looked extremely old and very heavy, which could explain why it was still standing. There were a few books left on the shelves. The rest of them were strewn across the floor. It was as if the Disciples thought the Affinites might have written down Gayle Mendosa's location and hidden it between the pages of one of their books.

Nathan scanned the state of the place, the light from his torch gliding over the furniture. To his right was a large white kitchen which looked out across the garden at the back. In the kitchen all the cupboards had been pulled open and their contents spilled out over the counters and floor. The chairs of the breakfast bar had all been flipped over and even the door of the oven was wrenched off.

"Over here."

Nathan turned his attention to his left. The living room must have been beautifully decorated once. One large midnight blue U-shaped sofa spanned the entire width of the floor-to-ceiling windows. On the wall to Nathan's left hung a large plasma television. But none of the likely very expensive furniture or paintings were what drew Nathan's attention.

Within the U of the large sofa were two chairs. One of the two was still standing, and a man was sitting on it; or rather was *tied* to it. The other chair had fallen onto its back, and there was another man strapped to it as well. There was blood pooling underneath both chairs.

"Over here!" Matu shouted again, but louder now so that the other three Asters could hear.

Nathan hurried quickly towards the two chairs and the men tied to them. The head of the man in the chair that was still upright was hanging forward. Nathan hoped the man was merely unconscious, but a roiling in his gut told him that hope was foolish. There was too much blood underneath the chair. The man was wearing striped pyjamas and Nathan didn't need to see the man's face to know that this was Logan Brown. The man on the floor was all in black. He was wearing a weapons belt, but there were no weapons attached anymore.

Nathan stepped towards Logan Brown while Matu examined the Italian Watcher on the floor. Nathan angled his torch towards the Australian Affinite. With cold precision he examined the extent of Logan Brown's torture and injuries. The man's white and blue striped pyjamas were stained in blood. Before doing anything else, Nathan brought his two fingers to right under Logan Brown's throat and waited.

There was no pulse. Nathan hadn't expected there to be one, but he didn't want to copy Sky and wrongly assume the man was dead when in fact he was clinging to life with every ounce of energy he had left.

At that moment a blue light flashed and Sky appeared in the room.

"There's no one upstai—" His words failed him as he took in the scene in front of him.

Nathan lifted Logan Brown's torn shirt and revealed the multiple stab wounds underneath. Nathan took a step back, pulled up one sleeve and shone his torchlight on Logan's arm. He saw that multiple gashes criss-crossed his arm all the way up to his shoulder.

Finally, Nathan reached and lifted the man's chin up and shone the torchlight into Logan Brown's face. No gashes there, as far as Nathan could tell. Only a lot of bruising and... Carefully Nathan dropped Logan's head back down. There had been a cracking feeling under his fingers as he had raised the head.

"They broke his jaw."

"They didn't expect him to speak, then," Matu muttered, looking up from the body of Lorenzo Benanti.

Sky stepped closer. "Their intelligence is pretty good. Orla Brown is in constant contact with Nelson. She is the sub-Emissary for the continent of Oceania; knows everything about every Affinite in Australia, New Zealand and the other smaller island countries like Fiji and Samoa."

"How do you know all this?" Matu asked.

Sky sucked on a tooth. There was no emotion in his voice as he spoke, but Nathan could practically feel the anger radiating off of him. "My mother is close to Orla."

It was unsurprising that Sky knew of Orla Brown. If indeed the woman had been such a prominent figure for the Affinites of this continent, it was to be expected that she would be close to the Aster line originating from here.

Lian and Sophie emerged from the stairs and beheld the scene. "The study's been ransacked. We hardly got started when you called," Lian said. "What've you got?"

"Logan was tortured. Benanti wasn't; quickly killed by something bigger than a dagger, judging by the amount of blood," Matu said, getting back up to his feet.

Sophie moved closer to examine the body of the Watcher for the source of the bleeding. "Not surprising. Watchers are trained to withstand torture, and they naturally have little connection to the people they are ordered to protect. Why else do you think these Australians were protected by Watchers from Peru and Italy? Felix has Australian Watchers, too." She paused. "What the..."

"What?" Sky asked.

"This is no ordinary kill."

"Which means what?"

Sophie was staring thoughtfully at the Watcher's blood-stained shirt. "Usually when a Disciple has no use for an Affinite, they keep it simple. A stab wound like Soto, or slashing a throat. Clean and quick. Look at this—" She lifted Benanti's shirt to reveal a horrifying scene in the torchlight. Just under his rib cage there was a massive trauma site. It was almost as if the Italian had been cut in half, only whatever blade had been used hadn't been wide enough to make a clean cut of it.

"Only one weapon does that: an axe," Sophie announced.

Nathan's insides turned even colder. He saw how the Watcher had been killed then. Strapped to the fallen chair, Benanti's chest had been exposed and unprotected when whoever it was had raised the axe and brought it down. The blade hadn't been wide enough to cut across Benanti's entire body, but it had cut through everything in its path. From where Nathan was standing, he could see the sliced organs and part of the man's spine.

But that wasn't the most chilling part of Sophie's announcement. There was one King in particular who specialised in using axes as weapons. Double-bladed axes in particular.

"That would mean..." Sky started.

"We don't know that for sure," Sophie snapped.

"*Soph*, even I know which King has made that weapon his specialty," Sky pushed.

"Exactly. *Everyone knows that*," Sophie emphasised.

"What are you saying? Any King could've done this to make us go after the wrong King?" Matu asked.

Sky exaggerated a sigh. "Can't we just find a clue, draw a conclusion and move on?"

"If only it were that simple," Sophie said sharply, unamused by Sky's flippancy. She looked up from Benanti's body. "Orla and Eli are still missing?"

"Seems like it," Nathan replied coolly.

A phone started ringing.

"Hang on," Matu said, digging into his jacket pocket and pulling out his mobile phone. "Axel? Soto and Benanti are dead, so is Logan Brown. Soto's body has already been sent back. Orla and Eli are nowhere to be—what?"

The other Asters stayed quiet as they watched Matu listen to whatever Axel had to say.

"We're on our way." Matu took his phone away from his ear. The Aster of Strength faced his siblings. "Another family in this time zone hasn't sent through their signal. The Jasman family in Makassar, Indonesia. They weren't a high-risk family; haven't been in real contact with the Small Council since Amisha's husband, Taman, passed away seven years ago. No Watchers were posted."

The Asters exchanged glances as Matu started tapping the screen of his phone, and then tossed the phone to Sky, who caught it easily. Nathan looked over Sky's shoulder and found that Matu had opened up a world map on his phone, which was now focused on a specific area. No street seemed to be nearby, just a footpath. Sky zoomed out and back in once to make sure he knew where he was going.

"You, Sophie and Lian go and see if anyone is still there. Nate and I will join you after we've finished searching here," Matu ordered.

"You've got my blood?" Sky asked.

Nathan patted against the small vial on the inside of his jacket, nodding once.

Sky nodded back. Sophie and Lian stepped beside him and each placed a hand on Sky's shoulder. Sky was still looking at the screen in his hands when the blue light appeared and the three of them vanished.

"So they don't have their information up to date after all," Matu muttered.

"Is Axel setting up a new protocol?" Nathan asked. The two of them turned their attention back to Benanti's body and started working on the rope that tied him to the chair. It had taken years of practise, but Nathan could shut out the horrible smell coming from the bodies, and it no longer did anything to him, seeing what had been done to them.

"Uh-huh," Matu said. He handed his torch to Nathan, so he could use both of his hands. He unsheathed the knife at his belt and cut through the rope, not bothering to try and untie it. "Every family that has even been in close contact with the Small Council or any of the other Islands' Councils are now at high-risk. Now that even the Watchers don't seem to be helping I expect many of them will be arriving on Saluverus soon."

"Do you think Josephine will be coming, too?" Nathan didn't stop to wonder if this was a question Matu wanted to hear. They were out on a mission and emotions never got in Nathan's way. Though Nathan knew Matu would already be thinking about what all this meant for his girlfriend.

"She might not," Matu said through gritted teeth. "Even though her mother is one of the highest-ranking Watchers for the Small Council she has no open contact with Axel as far as anyone outside of Saluverus is aware. She might think retreating to Saluverus could blow her cover."

Nathan could hear the concern in Matu's voice. It was true. Eileen Stewart was one of the most respected Affinites in the world. She had an affinity for sensing darkness and light, and usually wound up detecting an uprising before any of Saluverus' sensors picked it up. Eileen and her daughter Josephine were on Saluverus often. Josephine had been introduced to the Asters years ago. She was already close friends with Sophie when she started a relationship with Matu.

In theory Nathan understood Eileen's possible breaking of cover if she were to retreat to Saluverus right at this moment. But that didn't stop him from wondering what it would do to his brother to find Eileen dead on a chair and Josephine missing in the Underworld somewhere. Nathan knew for certain that Matu had already thought about that scenario. And now that the two of them were on a different continent than Africa, the scene of the first attack, and their siblings were on yet another continent, it was safe to say they had no clue which King was behind this.

The deathblow caused by an axe was their only clue...

But Sophie was right. That could be a false lead. They would only know for sure if they had a look at the exact weapon.

Once Matu had cut through the rope, he held it up in front of him and Nathan angled the torches towards it. Matu swore in Swahili and threw the rope away.

"Regular rope," Nathan observed. Disciples and Kings usually made everything themselves. Each weapon or object had *something* that indicated in which territory of the Underworld it had been made. Even rope, surprisingly. Nathan remembered at least three different kinds of rope that were used for torture and hanging that were made in the territories of the various Kings.

That was why seeing the actual axe used to kill Benanti was crucial. Using any axe to lead the Asters to the wrong King was easy. Stealing and using the actual weapons from that King with its specific markings and gemstones to give a false lead? That was well-nigh impossible.

"They know what they're doing," Matu grumbled.

Nathan gave Matu's torch back to him. "I'll go and look around. See if one of them dropped a weapon." He doubted it, but he didn't want to leave any stone unturned. The fact that neither of the Watchers could get any information back to Felix Hauser before getting attacked said something about the planning that had gone into the attack. The thought. The precision. The odds of one of the attackers leaving behind a weapon was small. Next to nothing. The Disciples had known of the Watchers. They *knew* that after the Okoth family in Kenya there would be extra precautions set up by the Small Council to try and track down which King was responsible and in which Underworld territory the abducted Affinite parents and children would be held captive. It was a good plan, attacking on each continent. The only problem was that, just like Reth Okoth, Orla Brown also had no idea where Gayle Mendosa lived. That was the one small mercy the Asters had going for them right now.

Nathan finished investigating the kitchen. There was nothing unusual about the ransacking of that room. All the doors had been pulled open so forcefully that half of them had one or both of their hinges broken. Kitchen knives and smashed crockery were all over the place. There was blood on the counter and the floor there, too. Nathan had no idea what state Orla and her son would be in. He didn't let himself think about how the two of them were forced to watch while Logan Brown was being tortured and Benanti was being killed.

Nathan let his mind go blank as he descended the stairs. He wondered what he would find on the ground floor, if anything. He wondered what the rooms were used for, since the living room and the bedrooms were on the middle and top floors. Lian had said something about a study being ransacked.

The answer came soon enough. At the bottom of the stairs Nathan stepped into the hallway. There was an open glass door in front of him. He shone his torch through it, only to find the study. Or what used to be one. Tall wooden cabinets spanned two of the four walls. A large desk stood underneath the large window with a computer on top. The keyboard of said computer was lying somewhere on the ground, together with hundreds and hundreds of loose pieces of paper. All the cupboards had been ripped open. Plastic folders that were used for sorting had been emptied and discarded on the floor, along with several ring binders and maps, all open and paged through.

Nathan pushed the glass door open and stepped into the study. The paper under his feet crunched as he moved through the room. He reached for one of the cupboards and pulled open the half-broken door. Nathan didn't find anything inside. Literally everything had been thrown onto the floor.

After a few minutes Nathan realised there was nothing in the study that would help him figure out from which territory these Disciples had come. He stepped back out into the hallway and looked over to his right. The door leading to the back room was open. It was a small room that, by the looks of things, had been turned into a home gym. By the light of the streetlamp outside, Nathan could just make out a cross trainer and a rack filled with different sizes of weights. The gym seemed to have been left alone. With how the living room and probably also the bedrooms looked, Nathan would have expected that at least the weights would have been thrown across the room.

Then something snagged his attention.

Nathan narrowed his eyes and started to walk towards the home gym room. There was something that reflected in the light of the moon as the clouds parted for just a moment. Nathan moved to the door and opened it further. In the doorway, he sank down to a squat to see what had caught his eye.

Right beneath the rack of weights was a weapon. The bottom of the hilt was silver and the hilt was mostly black. Ever so thin red lines wrapped themselves around the black hilt of the double-bladed axe. Even from this distance, Nathan could see the red stone in the centre in between the two blades, and the red carvings on the blades themselves.

They no longer needed to speculate which King was responsible.

Nathan stepped forward, ready to go and retrieve the axe so that Sophie or someone from the Small Council could confirm the same conclusion he had about its origins, when suddenly he noticed something else.

The second he stepped into the room, a little red light by his feet started flashing. At first the light was flickering slowly, but it didn't take long before the flickering started to speed up. Without a second's thought, Nathan raced out of the room, into the hallway and up the stairs.

"Matu!" he screamed as he fumbled for the vial of Sky's blood in his jacket pocket, dropping his torch in the process and running up the stairs in complete darkness. He didn't have time to do it carefully; he put the vial to his lips and took a whole gulp of his brother's blood. It tasted metallic, and Nathan winced as he swallowed.

Nathan dashed up the stairs and into the living room. Matu was staring at Nathan with a mixture of confusion and shock.

"*Excipe magica celeritatis!*" Nathan exclaimed as he reached his brother. There was a tingling on his skin and a replica of Sky's Band with the symbol of an angel's wing on the inside appeared on Nathan's wrist right next to his own.

Matu didn't resist as Nathan clasped a hand around his wrist and focused on the foreign magic now pulsing through his veins. He didn't know exactly where in Indonesia the others were, so Nathan merely forced the magic to find the person it officially belonged to, and hoped it worked.

The last thing Nathan saw before the blue light filled his vision was an orange flash, and he and Matu vanished just in time before the triggered bombs went off that would destroy the entire house.

Chapter 9

It was quite an adjustment from the luxury home in Perth, Australia, to the jungles of Indonesia. Sophie blinked, but saw nothing in the darkness. She reached for her torch and turned it on.

They were on the very outskirts of Makassar; she knew that much. She remembered being told about the Jasman family a few years back. Amisha and Taman Jasman had two children: Citra and Banyu. There was quite an age difference between them, Sophie seemed to remember. Amisha had found out about her second pregnancy after her husband had died. Sophie couldn't recall what had killed him.

Sophie angled her torch towards the house in front of her and started walking towards it. It was more a cottage than a house. It was made entirely of bamboo. The windows were open; they contained no glass, so the Disciples wouldn't have had to put in much effort to break in.

There were no other houses in sight. The cottage was completely surrounded by the jungle, with a single path leading up to the front door. Sophie guessed the nearest home would be at least a mile away.

It was hot and sticky here, even though the sun had set hours ago. Beside Sophie, Sky slapped himself on his neck and swore. Tiny insects were flying around them, attacking them at will. Sophie attempted to bat them away as she, Sky and Lian hurried up the stone steps that led up to the front door.

Sophie tried to push it open, and found that it was unlocked.

"That is not safe," Lian murmured.

"There are easier ways in than through the door," Sophie said as they stepped inside. She shone her torch to her left, illuminating the open space in between the bamboo frame where they would've expected glass windows to be.

"They really should've put in more effort to secure the house," Lian said.

Sophie looked around the silent space. "Amisha hasn't had anything to do with the Council for almost ten years. Disciples don't go rogue anymore to kill random Affinites. She thought she was safe."

"Well, she certainly wasn't," Sky said. He had taken off in a different direction to Sophie and Lian. The bamboo house was an oval shape. In the middle of the space in front of them was a staircase, which probably led up to the bedrooms. Lian and Sophie had gone to the left side of the staircase, finding three bamboo chairs around a small bamboo table. Small red cushions were still on the chairs, untouched. Sophie allowed herself the time to look at the two picture frames that were standing on the low table. In the left-hand frame was a photograph of the Jasman family after Taman's death. There were three people in the photograph: a girl of about fifteen years old with dark brown hair was standing next to a young boy about the age of eight. His dark hair was cut very short. And Amisha Jasman, their mother with long straight hair as black as night, was standing above them, her arms draped around her children's shoulders. All three of them were smiling at the camera.

The right-hand picture was a portrait photograph of Taman Jasman. His shoulders were relaxed and his chin was raised. He looked like a proud and serious man, even though he was smiling at the camera.

Sophie looked away and followed Lian. On the other side of the staircase was a small kitchen. There were two countertops, a fridge and an oven. So even though they lived with minimal supplies and in the jungle, the Jasman family still had electricity.

"Over here!"

Sophie and Lian hurried around the corner towards where Sky was standing. Immediately they understood what he meant by Amisha not having been safe. On the floor, strapped to a chair that had fallen over, was a woman. Sophie didn't need to check the woman's pulse to know that she was dead. She had a similar horrific wound to Benanti back in Perth. Across her chest, under her rib cage, a great force had cut straight through her body. Sophie didn't need to examine the wound to know that this was again inflicted by an axe. Either someone was really trying to lead them to start a fight with the wrong King, or the King in charge of these attacks was finally making himself known.

Sophie hoped for the former. She wanted nothing to do with the King whose signature weapon was the double-bladed axe, if she could avoid it.

Next to her, Lian swore as he saw the damage done to the woman on the floor. Sky muttered something under his breath. Sophie shook her head. They were too late again. Again they had walked in hoping to help, only to find a body instead. This time the body of a woman. A woman with wavy hair that in the torch light seemed more brown than black, and...

Sophie frowned. She looked down at the woman on the floor. She shone her torchlight at the woman's face. The woman *did* have brown hair. And it wasn't straight, it was wavy.

"That's not Amisha Jasman," Sophie realised out loud.

Sky looked up at Sophie, back to the woman, and then back again at Sophie. "What?"

"That's not Amisha." Sophie rushed to the other side of the small bamboo cottage. She snatched the picture frame off the table and hurried back to where her brothers were still standing in the same spot.

"Look." She held out the picture frame for both Lian and Sky to see. Her brothers strained their necks to see the photograph. Sky then turned back to the woman at his feet, knelt beside her and pulled some of the brown hair away from her face.

In that moment Sophie knew it for sure. The nose was different. Amisha's was smaller and pointier than the nose of the woman lying before them. And the mouth. Amisha's was thinner. This woman in front of them had fuller, thicker lips.

The woman before them was not Amisha Jasman. And still this woman had been bound to the chair and tortured before she had been gruesomely killed. Sophie hadn't failed to see the other cuts along the woman's arms, and the bruising on her face.

Lian grunted. "Then where the hell is Amisha Jasman?"

"And where the hell are her kids?" Sky added.

"Just... see if you can find anything on her body, or maybe the ropes, that can tell us anything—"

"She was killed by an axe, wasn't she? Doesn't that say enough?" Sky interrupted.

Sophie cast him a pointed look. "We're not jumping to conclusions *again*, all right? If this hadn't happened you'd be running around in the African Underworld right now."

Lian's head shot up. "*What?*"

Sky narrowed his eyes at Sophie. "*We*," he reminded her.

Sophie ignored him. She turned to Lian who was staring at Sky with a mixture of confusion and surprise. "Go and look around outside, maybe one of the Disciples dropped something. Sky, call Axel and then do a full sweep of this floor. I'll look upstairs, see if anything was disturbed there."

Lian and Sky responded with sounds of agreement before turning to their individual assignments. As Sophie headed for the stairs she heard Lian whisper, "Africa?" and Sky snap back, "*Let it go.*"

Then she heard Sky typing in a number on his phone – or maybe it was Matu's phone, since Sky still had that one, too. As she ascended the stairs, she heard Sky talking to Axel about the woman they had found. She was soon out of earshot and wouldn't be able to hear who the woman was who had unluckily been in the wrong place at the wrong time.

When Sophie reached the top of the stairs she stepped onto a tiny landing. It wasn't even large enough to fit two people. In front of her, and on either side, were doors. Three in total.

Sophie opened the door in front of her first, and found that it was the bathroom. She shone her torch inside and saw that nothing had been touched. The bath towels were neatly folded and the drawers under the sink hadn't been ripped open like they had been in the Brown and the Okoth houses.

Sophie closed the bathroom door and opted to open the door on her right. This was the master bedroom, as far as it could be called that. There was a small double bed on one side of the room, and a very crooked, single bamboo bed at the foot of it. Both of the beds were empty and had ruffled sheets, which meant they had been slept in recently. Sophie moved around the room, shining her torch every which way she looked. Next to the door was a single cupboard that Sophie assumed was used for clothes. Unlike downstairs and the bathroom, the bedroom did show signs of a struggle. The nightstand next to the double bed had fallen over, taking everything that had been on top with it.

Sophie bent her knees and picked up a broken picture frame. She turned it around in her hand and looked at the photograph within. Two women were standing next to each other; each of them had an arm draped around the other. Sophie recognised the woman on the right immediately as Amisha Jasman. It took her a little while longer to recognise the other woman. But once Sophie took in the slightly bigger nose, the wavy brown hair and the thicker, fuller lips, she knew.

Whoever the woman downstairs was, it was the same woman as in this picture. Amisha knew this woman, and knew her well.

Sophie looked at the room again. A double bed and a single bed...

Sophie had automatically assumed that the single bed was either for Banyu or Citra, one of Amisha's children. What if she was wrong...

Sophie leapt to her feet and left Amisha's bedroom. She opened the third door and found a second bedroom, with two single beds. Both empty, but only one of them had its sheets ruffled. The other bed was still made up. Three people had been sleeping in this house when the Disciples had broken in, while there should have been four. Sophie looked down at the photograph in the broken picture frame she realised she was still holding. There was something about the two women. They had the same eyes; not only in shape but also in colour. And the ears, and the shape of their heads... Sophie would bet anything that it was Amisha's sister who was lying on the ground downstairs.

Sophie was about to go down and tell Sky what she had discovered when she heard something. It had been so soft that she wondered if she had imagined it. Sophie narrowed her eyes and scanned the room silently.

There it was again. A sort of shift in movement. Like a foot sliding over the ground. Something...

Sophie shone her torch into the room. The two bamboo beds stood higher above the ground, but there was no way of looking underneath them. The sheets draped over the sides all the way to the ground. Sophie moved closer to the made-up bed, which was closest to where she had heard the sound. She crouched down, lifted the sheets and tossed them onto the bed.

She was met with a wall of bamboo.

She could've sworn she'd heard something coming from underneath...

Sophie scanned either side of the short bamboo wall that held up the bed and found what she had been looking for. At the bottom right corner of the short end of the bed was a little hole. It was no larger than a single finger, and anyone else would've missed it if they hadn't been looking for it specifically.

Sophie put one finger into the hole and tugged. The slab of bamboo came away without any effort at all, revealing a whole space underneath the bed. Sophie took a steadying breath, wondering what she would find in the secret space. She leaned down to get a look at the inside and gasped.

A small boy, no older than eight, was huddled all the way at the other end. His eyes were full of fright as Sophie shone her torchlight on him.

"Banyu?" Sophie whispered.

The boy shook violently and tried to crawl even further away from her.

"I'm not here to hurt you," Sophie said softly.

Banyu's bottom lip trembled and he made no move to come towards her. Sophie switched her torch to her left hand so she could free up her right.

"Do you see this?" Sophie asked, shining the light on the Band around her right wrist. "Do you know what this means?"

Banyu's eyes widened slightly, and whispered, "Aster?"

Sophie smiled at the boy and nodded. "That's right. I'm an Aster. I'm not going to hurt you. I'm here to protect you."

There was confusion on Banyu's face, and Sophie realised that the boy must still be learning English and wouldn't understand most of what she was saying. Sophie dug into the part of her magic where she could access languages and the Band on her wrist started to pulse with a golden glow. She then pointed at herself and said, in Indonesian, "My name is Sophie."

Sophie then pointed at Banyu and added, "Your name is Banyu, right?"

She waited for the boy to nod his head. "You can call me Sophie," she said in the boy's native language."

"Sophie," Banyu whispered.

Sophie nodded, trying to give the boy an encouraging smile. She gestured for him to come towards her. "It's okay, you can come out now."

The Band on her skin tingled as she spoke in a language that wasn't her own. Banyu seemed to understand that there wasn't any danger anymore, and even though the boy still quivered from head to toe, he started to move.

"That's right. Good job," Sophie encouraged.

A sudden crash downstairs had both of them freezing in place. Sophie whipped her head round towards the bedroom door.

"Sophie!" Sky yelled from downstairs.

Another crash.

Sophie snapped her head back to Banyu, who had already retreated all the way to the back of the space under his bed. He had started crying and shaking almost uncontrollably.

"Good, that's good." Sophie tried to sound reassuring. "Just stay there, okay? Stay there and don't move. Just like before, okay?"

She didn't give Banyu another glance as a third crash sounded downstairs. Sophie quickly grabbed the slab of bamboo and closed the bottom of the bed again. As carefully as possible, she brought down the sheets again so that nothing about Banyu's bed seemed out of place. Nothing about it that might have an intruder wondering if there was something suspicious underneath.

Sophie could hear someone climbing the stairs, so she sped towards the landing to meet them.

A female Disciple, recognizable by the signature brown fighting leathers, was almost at the top of the stairs when Sophie took a hold of either side of the bannister, and swung her legs forward. Her feet met the Disciple's face with a crunch. Sophie knew she had broken bone.

Having lost her balance, the Disciple fell backwards down the stairs. Sophie darted after her, unsheathing the rapier at her belt as she did so. Halfway down the stairs Sophie found that the female Disciple had landed on another Disciple who had been coming up the stairs behind her.

The two of them were about to get back to their feet when Sophie did the exact same thing again: she grasped the railing on either side and swung her legs forward. She connected with the female Disciple again, but the male one behind her caught Sophie's foot and pulled her towards him. Sophie lost her grip on the railing and fell hard on her back on the bottom few stairs. Pain shot through her back.

The male Disciple loomed over her, just as the female Disciple started to regain her footing. The male Disciple was holding a single sword and was about to drive it down into Sophie's chest. He brought the sword down, but right at the last second, Sophie spun sideways, missing the blade by inches.

The sword met bamboo with a sickening crunch.

In her scramble to get up onto her feet, Sophie swung her rapier-bearing arm around herself, slicing right across the side of the male Disciple's knee. He cried out and staggered back, just as the female Disciple started gaining on her.

Still in a crouched position and with pain searing up and down her back with each movement, Sophie raised her left hand to the female Disciple and pressed the small button. A tiny bolt shot out of the crossbow on her wrist and flew straight through her opponent's throat. A small click told Sophie that a new bolt had automatically slotted in to place.

The female Disciple clawed at her throat, but there was nothing she could do. She sank down to the ground as blood sprayed out of the wound.

Sophie pushed herself up to a standing position, her back throbbing as she moved. The male Disciple rose again, but having stumbled back when Sophie had caught his knee, he had no access to the sword he had attacked her with before. Looming over her, he reached for a weapon at his back.

Sophie planted her feet strongly at the bottom of the stairs and waited for the Disciple to come at her. She couldn't risk going to him and leaving the stairs exposed. She needed to keep any Disciple away from getting up the stairs and finding Banyu.

For a moment, Sophie's heart stilled as she took in the weapon the Disciple had just drawn from his back. She hadn't seen it until he revealed it in that moment.

It was a double-bladed axe. With red swirling decorations on the hilt and a red stone in the centre in between the two blades. A sudden cold spread through her body. She knew which King this Disciple served, and it wasn't good.

The Disciple lifted his arm up into the air and brought the axe down. Sophie saw it coming and blocked the blow easily. Even though her rapier was far less strong that the double-bladed axe, she only needed it to redirect the blows enough not to touch her. Sophie swallowed, ignoring the stabbing pain in her back as the Disciple tried again. Her jump was more like a stumble as she moved to the side, just in time to avoid another blow.

Each time their blades clashed it gave Sophie a fleeting chance to look around her. There were more Disciples in the house. Two were lying dead on the floor in the kitchen and one was on the upside-down dining room table. Another double-bladed axe with the same red lines was lying discarded close by.

Sophie let the male Disciple get two more blows in. Out of the corner of her eye she saw another male Disciple advancing with a knife in his hand.

The Disciple in front of her brought the axe down again. Sophie blocked it, then gritted her teeth and used all her strength to push the Disciple a few feet away from her. It was enough space for her to be able to shoot him with another one of her bolts.

Sophie frowned at the double bladed axe in the Disciple's hand as she raised her left hand, ready to shoot. Even with her weakened because of her fall, it hadn't taken much of her strength to push this Disciple away from her. And yet he was carrying this incredibly significant weapon. As far as Sophie had always known, only inner circle members and the King himself carried them. Not random foot soldiers, which this Disciple clearly was. It was like this King was screaming at them which Underworld he ruled. What on earth was he playing at?

Sophie didn't have the time now to question it. She pressed the button on the side of her index finger and the bolt shot the Disciple right in the heart. The Disciple stumbled back, and Sophie shot at him another two times to make sure he wouldn't be able to come back and attack again.

Sophie didn't have a lot of time to recover. The next Disciple was taller and stronger. Shooting the other Disciple another two times had given him the opportunity to get up close. He flung his arm towards Sophie with his single knife. Sophie dodged it, but found her shoulder grasped in his strong, free hand's grip. Sophie struggled. She dropped her rapier so that she could clasp her hands around his knife-bearing hand. Sophie growled as she put all her energy into keeping that hand with the knife in it away from her own throat.

The Disciple's face was so close to hers that she could smell his breath. Sweat was streaming down his face in the heat of the Indonesian jungle, as he, too, was using all his strength to get his blade to cut through her skin. Sophie knew she wouldn't be able to stop him. Her magic didn't give her extra strength. If she wanted to beat this man, she would have to do it another way. She would never be stronger than a male fighter; so, she would have to be smarter.

Sophie risked her balance to lift her foot and kick the Disciple hard against his knee. The Disciple balked and stumbled slightly. It was enough of an advantage. He had loosened his grip on her shoulder and his knife-hand had retreated away from her face. Not too far, though, but far enough so that Sophie could reach for the dagger at her belt and free it. When the Disciple regained his focus, Sophie was already swinging the dagger. In one quick movement that had her back barking, she sliced it across his chest.

Blood sprayed across her face and clothes as the male Disciple went down. Sophie stumbled back and steadied herself on the bannister behind her. Her back was screaming, and the heat of the jungle was tiring her out quicker than she was used to. She gasped for air and coughed once before scanning the room. Lian was in combat with two Disciples at once, while Sky was nothing more than a blue flash. One moment he was to Sophie's left, stabbing one Disciple in the belly with his short spear, and next he had vanished and appeared behind Lian, cutting down a Disciple before he could do any damage to his brother.

Sophie wanted to go to them; she wanted to go to Lian so she could fight back-to-back with him. She could see blood running down the side of his temple, but couldn't tell how bad the damage was. Worst case, Lian could get dizzy and disorientated soon if he had been badly hit on his head. Sophie needed to heal him quickly just in case, but she couldn't move away from the bottom of the stairs. There was only one way up and one way down, and she would make sure that no one even came close to finding Banyu.

"Sophie, get over here!" Sky shouted at her when he appeared once more close to Lian. Sophie understood what he wanted; in his eyes there was nothing more they could do here. Amisha and her two children were clearly not here, and what these Disciples were wearing and the weapons that most of them were fighting with was enough to tell them which King they were dealing with. It was better just to shimmer out and work from there.

But Sophie couldn't leave. She knew Banyu was upstairs, but she wasn't about to shout that across the room. Instead she gave Sky a hard look and shook her head to let him know she was staying put. She saw him frown at her before he disappeared again and attacked another

Disciple on Lian's right.

It was only then, looking at the space where Sky had been seconds ago, that Sophie realised that the lights had been turned on. And that same light illuminated the jungle outside, where even more Disciples were coming towards the bamboo house. It was a trap; two houses in the same time zone at the same time to split them up. They couldn't call Nathan and Matu; the two of them had no way of knowing that their siblings were in trouble. And Sky couldn't exactly leave to go and get them. The three of them would just have to hold these Disciples off long enough for Nathan and Matu to arrive here after they were finished with their top-to-bottom search of the three-story townhouse in Perth.

Sophie didn't want to think about how long that could take. Instead, she ignored the burning feeling in her back and prepared herself for another Disciple who had noticed her by the stairs. A second Disciple followed closely behind. Sophie pushed herself away from the bannister and picked up the axe the other Disciple had dropped at her feet. She allowed herself to forget everything around her. She gritted her teeth, raised the enemy weapon in her hands and engaged in battle.

When Nathan shimmered himself and Matu towards Sky and into the home of Amisha Jasman, he hadn't expected he'd shimmer right into the middle of a battle. It was carnage. There was fighting going on everywhere. Lian was in the kitchen, three Disciples dead at his feet as he engaged with another. His movements were slower than Nathan knew he could move, and he was bleeding heavily from a gash near his right eye.

Sky was a blue flash through the room. There were bodies of Disciples littered all over the place; by the sitting area, by the main entrance and by the dining room table. The moments when Sky would appear for longer than a few seconds, Nathan could see that his brother was tiring, too. His movements were less precise and he was gripping his short spear tighter than he usually did.

Sophie was near the staircase in the middle of the oval-shaped room. She was standing slightly bent forward, her shoulders hunched, as if her back was giving her trouble. Nathan could see that her clothing, although covered in blood, wasn't torn anywhere, which meant that whatever was hurting Sophie wasn't inflicted by a weapon, but by a blow or a fall.

Nathan didn't have much time to think. The second he had shimmered into the room, a Disciple near him discovered their sudden appearance and turned around to attack them. Nathan quickly reached for one of the broadswords at his back, but Matu was already in front of him, swinging his fists and sending the Disciple flying backwards and onto his back. Matu dived after him, the Band on his wrist blazing a bronze colour. As he went, he twisted his hand so the blade from his knuckle knife was pointing forward, and he dug the blade deep into the Disciple's chest.

Nathan heard a Disciple coming up behind him. He skipped backwards one step, which gave himself enough time to free one of the broadswords. That simple movement caused sweat to break out on his face immediately. The heat and humidity of the place was almost overwhelming.

When Nathan turned around, he found not one, but three Disciples heading his way. He took up a fighting stance and raised his sword up in front of him. Nathan barely registered the two Disciples coming in behind, as his attention was focused on the one in front that carried the weapon Nathan had hoped he wouldn't see here. Even in his cold, deadly state, Nathan felt the dread of facing that axe. He wasn't afraid of these Disciples. Their clothing alone suggested they were just foot soldiers, here to do some dirty work. No Disciple here was an inner-circle soldier as far as Nathan could tell. No, Nathan didn't fear this battle. But he did dread the implication of what this weapon meant. Which was probably precisely why a mere foot soldier had been given one for this attack.

Nathan brought up his sword and blocked the swinging axe of the first Disciple, and ducked away from the slashing sword of the second.

There was a blue flash and Sky had taken out the third. Nathan barely made out Sky's silhouette as the blue light of his shimmer took over and his brother was gone again. Nathan didn't have time to see where his brother appeared next; he was too busy fighting off the two Disciples at once.

Even though he had been fighting for less than five minutes, Nathan was already drenched in sweat. The air was filled with such clammy humidity here that it was hard for Nathan to keep a good grip on his sword. He moved away from another swing of an axe and brought his sword across and sliced one Disciple across his abdomen. The Disciple dropped to his knees, clutching his exposed and bleeding belly.

There was a loud crunch behind him, and Nathan knew that Matu had just crushed a Disciple's head with his bare hands.

"Sophie, get over here!" Matu commanded.

While blocking another attack with his sword, Nathan had just a split second to see that Sophie disobeyed Matu's order and remained by the staircase. Sophie caught Nathan's eye for a split second and he could see the pleading look in her eyes. She then looked up the stairs once before engaging with another Disciple again. Her body was shaking; her back was really hurting her. She wasn't even fighting back anymore. All her energy was going into blocking each blow as they came.

Nathan's eyes followed her look. Whatever the reason, Sophie did not want anyone getting to that next floor.

A yell from his right gave away another Disciple's attack, and Nathan moved aside gracefully, and brought his sword down on top of the Disciple's exposed neck. These really were grunt soldiers. They had put up a good fight against the three Asters already here; Lian was getting dizzy, Sophie was buckling under pain in her back and Sky was tiring. But with all five of them there, the Asters started gaining the upper hand, their magic playing a great part in that. The Disciples might even have succeeded if the bomb in the Perth townhouse had killed him and Matu.

Nathan didn't know how long he'd been fighting for, but soon enough the tide had turned and there were hardly any Disciples left standing. As Nathan cut down the last Disciple near him, his eyes shot across the room and he discovered that Matu and Lian were now fighting back to back, and Sky had stopped shimmering long enough to fight alongside Sophie. Nathan's lightning fast brother had understood the same thing he had, and was helping Sophie stop any Disciple from going up the stairs. They fought the Disciples off successfully, even though they were at a positional disadvantage; fighting side by side instead of back to back.

Nathan's gaze flew to his two brothers fighting in the kitchen, and saw that two Disciples had jumped out of the window and were running into the jungle thicket. Nathan dug into his magic and realised that these were the only two Disciples left in the area. No other ones had run away and no others were coming.

The Band on his wrist started pulsing green as he threw all his magic into the jungle around them. There was a screaming outside, and Nathan knew that his magic had worked. He hurried towards the kitchen counters, widely avoiding the Disciples Matu and Lian had just hacked to the ground, and looked outside.

Great, thick green vines had shot out from the ground and were very tightly holding the two retreating Disciples in place. Their weapons had been dropped on the ground, and the vines were growing thicker, pressing tighter around the two Disciples, like the slow strangulation of a python. Nathan willed his magic to slow down. They hadn't expected any Disciples to be in any of the raided houses. If they could manage to bring one back alive, they most certainly should take that chance.

Nathan looked over his shoulder and found Matu and Lian wiping their blades on their trousers. Sky and Sophie were doing the same. Sky was looking at Sophie and opened his mouth to ask a question, but Sophie had already turned and was racing up the stairs, not thinking for a second about if any of the Asters needed healing. Lian, as per usual, was hurt more than any of them. The idiot still didn't avoid blows as much as he probably should. Nathan noticed how he was holding on to one of the kitchen counters and had his eyes closed as if he needed to steady himself. His face was covered in blood.

Matu grabbed a tea towel from the counter and held it under the tap, before passing it on to Lian, who pressed it against the gash on his temple.

Nathan looked out of the windowless frame in front of him. "There are no more around."

He used his magic one more time to connect with the jungle outside, but the nature told him the same thing it had done minutes before. He wiped the sweat off his forehead and headed for the back door. Lian and Matu followed him.

"It's hot here," Matu said. "And clammy."

"You're telling me," Lian said. Their Japanese brother, who never seemed to look like he was sweating and rarely *ever* got any additional colour in his face after a tough workout, had an extremely red face and sweat was running down his neck like a waterfall.

"A lot of flies, too," Matu observed, slapping himself on the neck the second some sort of mosquito tried to bite him.

"Stop complaining. You only came in at the end," Lian said, a grin on his face.

"Sorry, got held up. Busy running away from a bomb," Nathan said matter-of-factly.

"*What*—woah…" Lian held out his free arm and swayed on the spot. Nathan jumped to his side and held on to his elbow to steady him.

Matu looked at Lian. "All right, you need Sophie. You've probably got a concussion. What do you feel?"

Even in his dizzy, disorientated state, Lian managed to chuckle and speak with such ease. "I feel nothing. Come on, brother, you know that."

Matu frowned at him. "You know what I mean."

Lian sighed and closed his eyes for a moment. "Well, my head is spinning and I can't seem to keep my balance."

Nathan knew Lian wouldn't say anything about a throbbing in his head, since that was one of the things Lian wouldn't be able to feel. The Band on his wrist was glowing silver, which meant it was keeping Lian from feeling any pain at all.

Matu studied Lian for another moment, but before he could tell Nathan to guide Lian back inside to find Sophie, Lian spoke again. "Look, it's not going to kill me in the next five minutes. Let's just finish this first."

Lian stepped away from Nathan's grip, swayed on the spot once more, but kept his balance. Nathan and Matu exchanged glances, but decided it was Lian's choice to make. The three of them walked a little further into the jungle to where the two Disciples were down on their knees, completely wrapped in green vines from knees to neck. Their faces had started to turn a little purple at the pressure and they were gasping for breath. Despite this, they were still doing their best to try and break free, both of them looking quite desperate when the three Asters stepped towards them.

Matu looked from one Disciple to the other. "We only need one."

He moved in front of one of the Disciples. His Band started glowing bronze. He then leaned down and swung his fist. With a horrible snap, Matu's fist met the side of the Disciples head, and because he was so completely wrapped in vines up to his neck, and there was nowhere else to go, the neck snapped.

Matu then turned to Nathan. "Can you keep him wrapped in that but still so he can shimmer back with us?"

Nathan nodded. The Band on his wrist started glowing green again, and he could feel his magic running through his veins. The vines around the Disciple that was still alive started shifting so that they were no longer wrapped around his legs. Only his torso now remained bound. A single short vine connected both ankles, so the Disciple could walk, but would fall if he attempted to run away. Another vine appeared around the Disciples chest, with a long loose end that fell at Matu's feet.

Matu frowned at Nathan.

Nathan shrugged. "Now you can walk him like a dog," he said matter-of-factly.

Beside him, Lian sniggered, while Matu closed his eyes, shook his head and smiled slightly. Nathan didn't exactly understand what was so funny. To him it was just a useful way of leading the Disciple around.

Matu leaned down and took the end of the vine. He looked at the Disciple and said, "Get up."

The Disciple gave Matu an ugly look and remained on the ground where he was. Matu rolled his eyes and sighed. "Fine."

He wrapped his hands around the top most vine around the Disciple's body. As his Band glowed a bronze colour, Matu seemed to hardly need any energy to pull the Disciple up onto his feet.

Once the Disciple was standing, Nathan took a knife from his weapons belt and held it at the Disciple's throat. "You might as well walk," he said coldly.

The Disciple glared at him, but didn't struggle when the three Asters started walking back towards the bamboo cottage. Knowing there was nothing he could do to escape, the Disciple trudged despondently along behind them.

Lian swayed a few times more, and even though he said he hadn't needed it, Nathan had taken his elbow again, to make sure he wouldn't fall.

Once they made it inside, Sky was heading back down the stairs. Nathan waited to see Sophie follow him down. He was wondering what they'd been doing up there, until he realised no one else was coming. The exhaustion Nathan had detected in Sky during the battle had gone. There were no more cuts and bruises along his arms anymore, either. Sophie must've already healed him.

"Where's Soph?" Matu asked.

"She found Banyu Jasman hiding in the false bottom of his bed," Sky explained. "Someone put in a lot of effort to keep him hidden, and it worked. I healed Soph's back with her magic and sent her and the boy back to Saluverus from up there; didn't think he'd want to see any of this—" Sky gestured to the twenty dead Disciples lying around the room. "Or *that*. What the hell is *that*?"

Sky had finally laid eyes on the Disciple behind Nathan and the others. Sky looked at Nathan with amusement all across his features.

"My new invention," Nathan said matter-of-factly.

Sky scanned the Disciple and his green prison from head to toe and nodded, a smile playing on his lips. "I like it."

"Let's get out of here," Matu said, tugging the Disciple closer to the four of them. The Disciple growled but said nothing further.

"Hang on," Sky said. He walked away from the kitchen, avoiding Disciple bodies as he made his way to the body of Amisha's sister. With a wave of his hand and a glow from his Band, the body vanished in a blue light.

As Sky walked back to his brothers, Matu leaned down to pick up one of the discarded double-bladed axes. "Axel is going to want to see this. No Affinite is safe for as long as Gayle Mendosa isn't on Saluverus. Axel needs to change his protocols immediately."

"And I need a doctor," Lian added. Somehow there was still amusement in his voice, even when his eyes fluttered and he lost his balance. Nathan stumbled slightly against the weight of his brother, but managed to keep both of them upright. Sky immediately jumped to Lian's other side to help. He wrapped one of Lian's arms around his shoulder. Matu stepped in closer, too, and placed a hand on Sky's arm.

Sky looked over to Nathan, who nodded at his brother, telling him he was ready to go. Within seconds blue light entered their vision and the four Asters and one Disciple were swept away from the hot and clammy jungles of Indonesia, and back to the October cold of Saluverus.

Chapter 10

Sophie and Banyu weren't in the Board Room when Sky shimmered in. Sky had already expected it; Sophie would've made sure Banyu went straight to the childcare centre.

Every member of the Small Council was in the room except for Sylvia Allen. Sky assumed that the Consul had gone with Sophie and the boy. The kid had never known his father. Now he had definitely lost an aunt, and quite possibly also his mother and older sister. Sky couldn't stomach the idea of going into the dining hall every morning from now on, and seeing that shaky, scared little boy at one of the tables with all the other orphans. The child had gone through enough. He shouldn't lose what was left of his family.

The members of the Small Council looked up as the four Asters shimmered in, the Disciple wrapped in vines in their midst.

Sky caught a glimpse of a smile on Axel Reed's face as the Ambassador beheld the Disciple trapped in Nathan's makeshift bonds. Axel was leaning against the chest of drawers by the window, but he pushed himself off the second his eyes found Lian, almost completely unconscious, being held upright by Sky and Nathan.

Sky strengthened his grip on Lian. "We need Sophie or her blood, now!"

Axel immediately headed for the small closet door. Before he entered it, he pointed at the Disciple. "Take him away."

Felix Hauser quickly moved to the wall of filing cabinets. He pulled one of the drawers open and took out a small plastic case. He opened the case, selected a syringe and walked over to the Disciple. The Disciple tried to step away from the Spymaster, but Jackson Kelly was already there, holding the prisoner in place. Felix stuck the needle into the Disciple's neck and, with his thumb, injected blue fluid into the Disciple's body. It took less than ten seconds for the Disciple's eyes to droop.

Felix turned to Nathan and nodded. The Band on Nathan's wrist started glowing and the vines vanished into thin air. Just before the Disciple lost consciousness completely, Jackson and Felix caught him, and carried him out of the room. They were no doubt headed for the dungeons in the basement. Or they would go straight to the static portals and take him to the Frozen Dungeons in Glacialis to interrogate him there.

The Board Room door closed behind them with a soft thud.

Axel re-emerged from the closet with a small glass with red liquid in it. Matu stepped forward and took it from him. Sky and Nathan both sank to their knees to lie Lian down on the floor. He wasn't completely unconscious; his eyes were still open, but they were glassy and unfocused.

Matu took a sip of Sophie's blood and spoke the incantation to harness her magic. "*Excipie magica sanitatis.*"

A Band just like Sophie's, with the staff of Caduceus on the inside, appeared next to Matu's own Band. Immediately it started glowing golden. Matu placed his right hand on Lian's temple and closed his eyes to concentrate.

Sky and Nathan waited and watched as the gash on Lian's forehead started to close. When Sophie did this, the healing was always faster than if any of the other Asters harnessed her magic. It was always an effort to use each other's magic, as it wasn't their own and therefore felt slightly unnatural.

When the gash near Lian's eye had closed completely, and only the leftover blood remained on his face, Lian's eyes shot open. He pushed himself up into a sitting position and looked around at the faces that were staring back at him. "That feels better," he said with a crooked grin.

Sky rolled his eyes and got back to his feet, pulling Lian along with him. As he turned to the Ambassador, he found that Axel was looking at Matu, Nathan and himself suspiciously. "None of you need any healing?"

Matu shook his head and gestured to Nathan. "We only came in at the end."

"And Sophie already healed me back there," Sky added.

Axel took one last, concerned look at each of them, before his face turned serious. "Good. Well, then." He returned to business. "The dead woman was Amisha's sister, Dara—"

"I've sent her body to the morgue," Sky interrupted.

Axel glanced at Sky and nodded in acknowledgment before continuing. "According to Nicholas, Dara had been staying with Amisha and her children for the past few weeks. Banyu is safely in the childcare centre while his sister Citra and his mother are still unaccounted for. Sophie said the attack in Makassar came from Disciples from the South American Underworld."

"Oh, they came from South America, all right," Matu said, taking the double-bladed axe he had secured in his weapons belt earlier and placing it on the oak table. Axel stepped forward and examined the weapon. Sky leaned over as well. He had been so in the zone during the battle, trying to keep Lian and Sophie alive at different ends of the bamboo cottage, that he hadn't given any thought to where the Disciples might have come from.

The Disciples that had killed the Italian Watcher, Benanti, and Amisha's sister, Dara, hadn't used a double-bladed axe just to put the Asters on the wrong track. They had not been trying to hide where they came from, at all. Sky stared at the intricate red design down the hilt of the double-bladed axe. That same design surrounded the glowing red stone in the centre between the two blades, as well. He had only ever heard of this weapon before, and by whom it was used. The sinister weapon with its signature design and colouring was enough to send a spike of worry through him.

"Sophie also mentioned that the Disciples you fought were nothing more than foot soldiers. Not a higher-ranked soldier amongst them. Would you say the same?" Axel asked.

All four boys nodded in agreement. The weapon might have slipped Sky's mind during the battle, but the level of skill the soldiers had shown hadn't been hard to miss. The Asters had fought highly ranked soldiers before, and these were definitely not that.

"Why would he give his foot soldiers axes? Those things are almost sacred down there," Lian said.

"To make absolutely sure we know which King is responsible for these attacks?" Sky suggested.

"Couldn't he just send a note?" Lian said.

Sky sniggered. "No, I would've preferred sky writing."

"That does have more flair," Lian agreed.

"Guys..." Matu warned. Lian and Sky both pressed their lips together to stop themselves from laughing.

Axel threw them a withering look, but did not answer Lian's original question. If he had ideas himself about the King's motives he clearly wasn't going to share them with the Asters.

"It's not for you to worry about for now. Do any of you have any more information that is of importance to us right at this moment?" the Ambassador asked instead, returning to the matter at hand.

"The attack on Perth was also by South American Disciples," Nathan said.

Axel turned to the Aster of Flora. "You are sure?"

Nathan nodded. "Benanti was killed by an axe and I've seen the weapon in the house. You can only trust my word. I can't get you proof."

It was no longer a surprise to Sky to hear Nathan speak so strongly to the Ambassador when he was in this state. Probably when they were dismissed and left the Board Room, was when Nathan would switch back to his quiet, kind self. Right now, he was still in that deadly, focused state.

"You can't get proof?" Axel repeated, questioningly.

Nathan shook his head. "The house blew up. There was no time. But there is no doubt in my mind."

While Axel nodded slowly, Sky spun his head towards Nathan. This was the first time he was hearing of the explosion at the Perth townhouse. Nathan didn't meet his gaze, however, so Sky looked over to Matu, who gave him a short nod before turning his attention back to the Ambassador.

"Anything else?" Axel asked.

The four Asters shook their heads.

"All right. We'll be sending in cleaners to the Brown's house and Jasman's cottage to clean everything up. We'll send in our stronger Affinite soldiers to oversee the cleaning of the Jasman cottage in case any Disciples are still lurking around."

Sky sniggered, knowing that Jacob Henderson would most probably be one of those Affinite soldiers. The odds that any Disciple was stupid enough to hang around was small. Sky could picture Jacob now: being sent through one of the static portals in the castle, just to stand around in that humidity and enjoy the lovely smell of decaying bodies while being stung by mosquitos.

Axel chose to ignore Sky. "We're working on new protocols. You will learn whatever new information Kelly and Hauser get from the Disciple in a few hours." Axel looked at his watch. "It's six p.m. now. You may do whatever you like until you hear from me. Make sure you eat and change. You are all dismissed."

In any other circumstance Sky might have taken this opportunity to joke about Axel's phrase of them being allowed to do *whatever they liked*, but even he knew that he'd joked around enough already, and that Axel had reached the end of his patience. Now wasn't the right time. A parent and a child from three Affinite families had been taken, and they had no way of finding out where they were. The only thing they now knew for sure was that they were in the South American Underworld, and not in the African one. Sky didn't want to think about his foolish idea to storm the African Underworld when the abducted Affinites had never actually been there. How those Disciples managed to get those Affinites to South America so quickly was anyone's guess. A King attacking Affinites on other continents hadn't happened for years; it had never happened in the time Sky and his siblings had been active Asters. So why were the other Kings allowing the South American one to do it? He was trespassing, and yet there was no retaliation, as far as they knew. Why?

Sky grunted as the four boys exited the Board Room. It wasn't their job to figure it out. Unless Axel specifically commanded them to do so, they would not involve themselves further in the case. Sophie might; Sky knew it would eat her up inside not knowing how the South American King had done it. She would want to know.

Without speaking, the four boys headed in the same direction.

The children's care centre was one floor higher on the eastern side of the castle. It was the side that wasn't inside the cliffs, but looked out over the island and the Norwegian Sea beyond. There were floor-to-ceiling windows that gave a panoramic view of Saluverus.

The centre took up three floors in one of the larger circular south-eastern towers. It didn't take long for the boys to find Sophie. She was on the middle floor, sitting at a small round table next to Banyu. Her Band was glowing golden. They were whispering softly to each other. Banyu smiled at something Sophie said.

Sky was glad to see the child had been given a thick jumper and that a blanket had been placed over his lap. Banyu had stopped shaking, at least, though he still looked extremely tense. His eyes flitted across the room at every sound and movement around him.

"Excuse me," came a voice behind them.

The boys all turned around to see a small, plump woman standing in the doorway, holding a steaming plate of food. Sky didn't recognise any of the ingredients aside from the rice. And it didn't smell anything like any food from Europe.

"Stop staring," Katina Ivanov, the Russian Affinite and head of the child's centre, said. "It's called pepes. Figured he'd rather eat something he knows."

She probably added the last bit of information at the sight of three of the four boys staring at the food as if it was utterly alien. Only Lian seemed to be unfazed by the pile of green-brown ingredients on the plate.

Katina shrugged as if it was the most normal business in the world. "That's what you get when you have children from all over the world come here. The kitchens have to be prepared for any cuisine, you see. And cutlery," she added in her high-pitched, chatty voice. She held up her other hand that was holding not only a knife and fork, but also a spoon and a set of chopsticks.

Katina stepped past the boys and was about to head over to Banyu and Sophie when she turned around. "Is there any reason for you to be here? Looking like that you might scare the children. Never mind *the smell.*"

Sky looked around the room and found that there were another four children between the ages of five and eight in the room. All four of them were staring at the four Asters, their eyes wide and their mouths forming an O.

Katina hurried along to the small round table and placed the food in front of Banyu. The boy's eyes grew wide and he gladly accepted the spoon amongst the cutlery that Katina offered him. The head of the centre then leaned over to Sophie and whispered something in her ear.

Sophie looked past Katina at the four boys, a smile growing on her face. Then she turned back to Katina, nodded, and whispered one final thing to Banyu, before standing up and heading towards the door. Katina took Sophie's seat beside Banyu to keep the boy company.

The four Asters went ahead of her and waited for her in the hallway.

"She wants us all to leave," Sophie told them.

"Yes, according to her, we stink," Sky said, acting offended on purpose.

Sophie wrinkled her nose. "She's not wrong."

The five of them headed through the castle's corridors, which were almost completely deserted. Most of the castle's inhabitants would be in their rooms after a hard day's work, or already in the dining hall for their dinner.

The Asters headed for their common room. They were in desperate need of a shower. They were still covered in blood and sweat from their battle in the Indonesian heat.

"What did you find out?" Matu asked Sophie.

Sophie looked across to her brother. "A lot, actually. The attack didn't happen all at once. The Disciples first went into his mother's room, where his Aunt had also been sleeping for the past few weeks. When his sister—"

"Citra, right?" Lian interrupted.

"Yes. So when Citra heard the sounds she forced Banyu to hide under his bed in the false bottom. She told him that he shouldn't come out, even if he heard something. Or heard nothing. She told him to wait until someone found him, and she hoped it would be one of us," Sophie explained.

"Smart girl," Sky mused.

"How old is she?" Matu asked.

"Fifteen."

"That's quite an age difference," Matu observed.

"Banyu wasn't planned. When Amisha found out she was pregnant it was soon after Taman had died. She doesn't believe in abortion, but even if she had, she wouldn't have done it."

"And you know this, how?" Sky asked.

Sophie shot him a *look* that told him enough. Sophie knew goddamned everything. Whether it was through a book or through her own magic. Sky never knew where her own research ended and her magic began.

"What else?" Matu asked.

"Citra told him she'd pretend he was sleeping over at a friend's house. Then she closed the fake bottom and left. From what I could see Citra was very smart indeed. She somehow even had the presence of mind to make up Banyu's bed to make it seem as though no one had slept in it that night. I assume the Disciples broke into their room right after that and took her downstairs to where her mother and aunt were already being tortured."

Sky let out a long breath.

"I know," Sophie sighed, knowing exactly what he meant with his sigh. "How has it come to this?"

"It feels like we're always a step behind," Sky muttered.

He saw his brothers nod beside him.

"Like it's been planned for so long, and we're only just catching up," Lian added. "But then I suppose they have had nearly eighteen years to do so."

"It doesn't feel like we're catching up, though," Sky almost growled. "We're running around and appearing exactly where they want us to, when they want us to. No action was our decision; we're only reacting."

"Do you want even more bad news?" Sophie asked.

Sky rolled his eyes to his sister. "Not really, but shoot."

"The Disciples that attacked us were from South America."

Sky shook his head. "So? Nate said the ones in Perth were, too."

Sophie's eyes flew open in shock at that piece of news.

"What?" Nathan asked. "What's so bad about that?"

Sophie sighed, obviously annoyed that none of the boys had any idea what she had concluded. "South America was Astaroth's territory."

"So? It's not anymore. He's dead," Lian said.

It was true. The worry Sky had felt at seeing those legendary axes he'd only heard about in stories and seen drawings of in books, had gone as quickly as it had come, because Astaroth was indeed dead. Ever since the war twenty-five years ago, which had concluded with Tomas Mendosa killing Astaroth, the only Original King left was Kirnon, the King of the Asian Underworld. But he had never been a real threat. No one had heard anything from his territory in decades. The Asian Underworld was practically a ghost town. But there was one other territory that they also hadn't heard anything from in years... actually they had never heard from that territory for exactly twenty-five years...

"Oh, crap," Sky said, realizing what Sophie had meant.

Sophie nodded at her brother in approval. "We have no idea who the King of the South American Underworld is."

"*Jahamanu*," Matu swore.

A Disciple born on the day of Astaroth's death would be born with the dead King's magic and would become the next King himself. Why they were always male, Sky had no idea, but they were. Usually after a new King was born, word got out quite fast. The Affinite Mergers in the Underworld got the news very quickly, and because of them, so did the Small Council and the Asters of that generation. But in the past twenty-five years there hadn't been any news on who the new King of the South American Underworld was. Absolutely nothing.

"So we have no idea what we're up against," Lian concluded, "or what kind of following this new King has."

"We know he has the same magic Astaroth did," Matu said.

"But we have no idea in what way he will wield it," Sophie said. "And if the Perth townhouse was attacked on the same King's orders, then I would bet anything it was also that King who ordered the attack on the Okoth family. There is only one King who has been daring enough to make a play for Gayle Mendosa and her magic, and it's a King we've never faced before."

"And know absolutely nothing of," Nathan added quietly.

They had made it to their common room and stepped inside. The fire in the large fireplace was burning fiercely, and it filled Sky's cold bones with warmth.

Sky shuddered once. "How the hell are we going to save those Affinites, *and* protect Gayle Mendosa at the same time?

Sophie opened her own bedroom door. "We're not." All four boys stared at her in confusion before she added, "Axel didn't tell you? Our parents are coming."

It was after they had finished their meals in the dining hall that the Asters were called back to the Board Room. At dinner, Sophie had explained to the others how Axel had planned to bring in the Asters of the previous generation, known now as Ceders, as back-up for their operation to keep Gayle safe, and the Affinites held in the Underworld from getting killed.

Sophie had only spoken to her mother on the phone less than a week ago. It was strange to think that both of her mothers would be coming in from London for the mission of all missions.

Sophie had been told her parents' love story a million times. Same-sex marriages had been approved of years earlier, yet it had still caused quite some commotion when Katherine Griffiths had arrived on Saluverus after a holiday, showing off her new Canadian girlfriend, Ivana. Sophie loved hearing the story of the Canadian country-girl Affinite falling for the famous Aster of Health and Knowledge. She never tired of hearing how her two mothers fought off prejudice and judgment, even against some of Katherine's fellow Asters at the time. Each time Sophie went home to London in weekends and holidays, she was reminded again and again that you should never give up a fight you know you want to win. Even if everyone at the time believed you shouldn't.

There had been questions at the time of how Katherine's magic would continue to live on. There were of course ways for Katherine to have a biological child, but the two women had decided to adopt instead.

Every Aster had the ability to pass on their magic once without losing it themselves, either through the birth of a child or through a spell. Most of the time that spell was used when an Aster died, to pass on the magic running through said Aster's veins, and place it into another living soul to carry on the lineage. In Katherine's case they used the spell when she was still alive. It had worked perfectly, and Sophie had gained the magic of Health and Knowledge; but from that moment Katherine would never be able to pass on her magic again. In the past there had been attempts to create more Asters with the same magic, but those had all ended in failure.

So, Sophie wasn't either Katherine or Ivana's biological daughter, but she felt it nonetheless. None of her brothers had ever given her a hard time about her home family being different than theirs. Even better, they would angrily stand up for her if anyone else showed her such disrespect. Though that hadn't happened in years, Sophie still clearly remembered Sky even going so far as breaking the nose of an Affinite who had made a small joke about *the adopted Aster with the lesbian mothers*. It had earnt him two weeks in detention, but Sophie had sat alongside him in the detention centre all that time in gratitude.

When the five Asters stepped into the Board Room they were met with a surprise: the four Ceders were already there. Madeleine Mayne, Sky's mother, stood tall and proud at the window, with her blonde hair hanging straight down past her shoulders and her blue eyes sparkling as she beheld her son walking in. It struck Sophie again each time she saw Madeleine, how much Sky looked like her: the same blonde hair, the same dark blue eyes; even the shape of their nose and mouth was similar. Madeleine was wearing a very chic, deep-blue pantsuit and black high heels. Obviously, she hadn't had time to change before being summoned there.

Diallo Madaki, Matu's father, stood next to Nicholas Nelson at the corner desk. The Ceder of Strength towered over the Emissary with his tall stature, broad shoulders and gigantic chest. Nathan's mother, Rose Radbourne, sat at the round oak table in the middle. It was hard to imagine that Nathan's tall, strong frame came from this small, delicate woman. Unlike Sky and Madeleine, Nathan and his mother had no features in common.

Sophie spotted her mother standing next to Madeleine at the window, and headed over to give her a hug.

"Good to see you," Katherine Griffiths whispered in her ear.

"You, too," Sophie whispered back. She then straightened and turned around.

Of all the Asters of the previous generation, only the Ceder of Speed, Strength, Flora and Health were here now. Yoshiko Fai, the Ceder of Analgesia and Lian's mother, had died a year ago, while Tomas Mendosa, the Ceder of Endurance, was of course away from Saluverus. There had never been an Aster of Endurance in the current generation because Tomas' child had been born the reincarnation of Queen Aiyana, and possessed her magic instead. Gayle Mendosa's parents were both Asters, but her mother didn't come from any of the six Aster magics that Aiyana had created five hundred years ago. Cara Mendosa was now the Ceder of Mind, and had become an Aster in a very unique way. But that was a whole other story.

Sophie went over to stand by Lian, who was unnecessarily confronted by the knowledge of his parents no longer being with them.

Axel Reed cleared his throat and everyone in the room turned to look at him. "Good to have you all here on such short notice."

Though the Ambassador was only a few years older than the Ceders they all had the utmost respect for him. They didn't complain about being summoned even though they were no longer the active generation of Asters. If they were called upon, it was for a very good reason, and they were never to doubt it. And they didn't.

Aside from Axel, only Sylvia and Nicholas from the Small Council were in the room. Jackson and Felix must still be in the Frozen Dungeons interrogating the Disciple Nathan had managed to capture in the jungles of Makassar.

"You have all been brought up to speed," Axel continued, addressing the Ceders. "No Affinite on the Surface is safe until Gayle is safely behind Saluverus' Curtain. New protocols have been set, and as of this moment, Affinites from all over the world will be coming here or to Viria or Auro, for protection. We have been in contact with Tomas and Cara and they have also been briefed on the new developments. It seems as though the new King of the South American Underworld is making his appearance at last. And although we know nothing about him, it won't change what we are about to do."

The room was utterly silent as he spoke. Sophie could feel the tension in those present. Her generation of Asters had never been involved in a mission this important before. Their parents had been part of a war and had seen the worst of what the truly evil, and most powerful King in history could do. Sophie had a horrible feeling they were just seeing the beginning of what that particular King's reincarnation was capable of.

"At three a.m. tonight, the Ceders will travel to Brazil and they will be accompanied by Percy Kelly," Axel continued. Surprised, Sophie turned her head and realised there was another man in the room she hadn't noticed before. He was standing against the wall of filing cabinets and looked creepily the same as Jackson. Sophie had never seen the man before, but his posture, the red-brown scruffy hair and the dark brown eyes were practically identical to his twin brother's.

For the past thirteen years Percy Kelly had been disguised as a regular martial arts sensei in the town Gayle Mendosa had grown up in. It had been one of the conditions set by the Small Council when Tomas and Cara Mendosa had decided not to raise Gayle on Saluverus. Even if Gayle wouldn't know about her magic until she returned here, she would at least already be a semi-professional when it came to combat.

Percy Kelly was as skilled a soldier as his brother. The two of them had become known as the best Affinite soldiers during the war against Astaroth, and had headed up the training programme of all Affinites and Asters on Saluverus since that war. Aside from Madeleine Mayne on occasion, Percy Kelly was the only one who travelled back and forth between Saluverus and Gayle Mendosa's home town in Brazil. He had been cloaked just like Tomas, Cara and Gayle were, so that no Disciple would ever recognise any of them if they happened to wander into their vicinity.

"Madeleine and Percy will meet the Mendosas on the edge of the town, while the other Ceders will watch the town for any signs of danger; Gayle will remain asleep and unaware in her house. This will be at eleven thirty p.m. their time. In this meeting you will discuss the plans for Gayle to travel here tomorrow afternoon. Timings and place need to be worked out. All the air routes need to be free, and everything needs to happen undetected. There must be no room for interception. We don't know how this new King is using his magic, but we do know the extent and limits of Astaroth's magic, so we work with those in mind," Axel explained.

Tomorrow.

Gayle Mendosa was arriving tomorrow.

The Queen was coming home.

It was no surprise that the Ceders were given this task. Just because Sophie and the boys were the active Aster generation, didn't mean that the Ceders were any less capable of doing these jobs. They might even be better in some circumstances; their powers had matured, they had even better control over their magic, and they had years of experience dealing with Kings and Disciples from all over the world.

This was the very first time Sophie and her generation of Asters would even face a King. Having the Ceders there to help with a mission as important as this one only made sense. But even with the Ceders' help, there were still so many things that could go wrong. Sophie just hoped that whoever this King was, he wasn't as unpredictable as he might think he was.

Axel continued explaining the rest of his plan. "In the meantime, the Asters will remain here. They will be helping with the arrival of Affinites until this evening, while being ready to be summoned at any moment. The ten o'clock signal still stands for the families not ready to leave before then. The scientists in Glacialis are continuing to develop a technology that can track Affinite essence in the Underworld. The technology should be live tomorrow afternoon, which is when you," he indicated the Asters with a nod of his head, "will head into the South American Underworld in search of the missing Affinites. We will make sure that the technology doesn't pick up the undercover Mergers already down there looking. We need to avoid blowing their cover at any cost."

Sophie's heart began to thump. Their scientists had created some-thing that would help them find the Affinites in the Underworld. *Finally.* Sophie had doubted Axel slightly until now. She knew the Ambassador must've been working on something, but it was good to hear it spoken aloud and that it was almost finished.

Sophie wished Axel would share more of his plans with them, but he was the Ambassador for a reason. He didn't need to tell the Asters everything about what he was planning. Sophie should've known that the scientists in Glacialis were already working on something. Aside from housing the Frozen Dungeons, Glacialis was most known for making all Aster and Affinite weapons in its factories. What was less known was that there were labs filled with scientists working on any number of innovations to help protect the Affinites and humans in the world; including, apparently, this tracking system.

Axel's final words sounded through the room. "That is all for now. You are all dismissed."

Tomorrow. Sophie didn't know if it was ever going to sink in.

Everything was happening tomorrow.

She and her generation would be going after the Affinites. And Gayle was coming home at long last. Sophie breathed a shaky breath. Everything was happening at the same time. Sophie wasn't quite sure if this was a good thing, or a very, very bad thing indeed…

Chapter 11

There hadn't been much time to catch up with their parents. Madeleine Mayne, Rose Radbourne, Diallo Madaki and Katherine Griffiths had almost immediately gone off with Percy Kelly and Nicholas Nelson to prepare for their trip to Brazil. They had to get their hands on some appropriate clothing and weapons, and they needed to make sure all their cloaking spells were up to scratch. If any Disciple detected their presence or their magic close to that small town near the Amazon Rainforest, then it would all be for nothing. They would know Gayle's location and the Ceders would then have a fight on their hands to get the unaware Queen out safely. The fact that the South American King was deploying his Disciples across other territories in a desperate last search for Gayle was in itself reassuring; the King was clearly completely unaware that Gayle had been living in his own backyard all these years.

There also hadn't been much time to discuss the plan Axel had laid out for the Asters. About what would happen when Glacialis' tracking device was ready for use. Less than fifteen minutes after the meeting in the Board Room, Affinites from all over the world had started arriving on the island, and the Asters were expected to help receive them.

There was an organised way to get them all there. There were static portals all over the world, usually hidden within the training academies in the larger cities. The portals in Asia and Oceania led to Viria in the Indian Ocean, and those in South America and the southern half of Africa went to Auro in the South Atlantic Ocean. The portals in North America, Europe and the northern half of Africa led to Saluverus. The Affinites coming through the portals to Saluverus would be appearing on the large courtyard in front of the castle, which was exactly where Sophie and the other four Asters were standing and waiting for them. It was a dry evening, but the cold ocean wind whipped around them mercilessly. Sophie shivered and pulled the zip from her coat all the way up to her chin. Sky was moving from side to side to keep warm, and everyone else had their hands shoved deep into their pockets.

Other Affinites working in the castle were there with them as one family after another appeared on the green lawn. Sophie was holding a clipboard and was crossing off the names of the families that had arrived. Behind each name was written the room number in the residential wing of the castle. The four boys and the other Affinite helpers each took a family inside and showed them where they would be staying, before coming back down to the courtyard and doing the same with the next family.

Sophie knew that it would take a while before all the families would get there; there were plenty of Affinite families who lived a long way away from the big cities that housed the academies and the static portals. The Affinites helping out and bringing the families to their rooms would be there all night. Axel had made it extremely clear that the families should travel there as fast as possible. It didn't matter what time it was on Saluverus; there was an urgency to keep the families free from danger for the next two days until Gayle was safely on the island. At that point many of the Disciples on the Surface would be expected to return to the Underworld, and the Affinites would be able to go back home.

Sophie and her brothers would've helped all night, too, if they didn't have their mission the following afternoon.

A bright light flashed in front of Sophie and a large family group appeared. Sophie recognised the head of the family immediately. Nadine

Amsel stood in front of her with her five children close around her. Nadine was a German Affinite, and Sophie knew of her because she had been one of Percy and Jackson Kelly's best soldiers in the war against Astaroth. She had since retired from fighting, and worked as a Watcher for Felix Hauser, operating out of her home in Berlin.

Sophie bowed her head to the former soldier and said, "Welcome to Saluverus."

Nadine Amsel nodded back. There was no kindness on the woman's face. She had probably thought she and her family were safe, but when news came that even an Affinite house closely watched by two of Felix's best Watchers had been ambushed, she knew she could be next. It didn't surprise Sophie one bit that the woman was here as one of the first families to arrive. There was no Mr. Amsel anymore. He had died of cancer only a few months after their youngest daughter, Amelie, was born.

Sophie looked over the children and turned her attention to the clipboard in her hand. She ticked off all the names of the Amsel family: Nora, the eldest at seventeen, Stefan and Hanno, the two sons at ages fourteen and seven. And finally, two more daughters, ten-year-old Lena and little Amelie, aged three. Sophie looked up from the clipboard. The entire family had flaming red hair, pale brown eyes and freckles covering their faces. Sophie wondered what, if any, genes had come from Mr. Amsel, considering that the children were complete replicas of their mother, in looks at least.

"Nathan will show you to your adjoining rooms," Sophie said, still smiling. Nathan came up to Sophie's side, and she added, "Rooms 126 to 128."

Nathan looked up at the Amsel family. "Follow me."

He leant in and offered to carry two of their suitcases. Nadine Amsel, who already had a bag slung across her shoulder *and* was carrying her three-year-old daughter, merely nodded and followed Nathan up the stone stairway to the main entrance of the castle. The rest of the family followed in silence. It didn't seem like any of them were particularly happy to be there.

As the afternoon turned to evening, Affinite families continued to appear in the courtyard. It was almost midnight before Sophie finally fell backwards onto her bed. She'd been in quite a bad mood ever since Jacob Henderson had shown up later on, just to hit on her and make fun of her brothers.

"Awh... the Asters are on welcome duty," he had scoffed, strolling onto the courtyard on his way back to his room. "What was the problem? Did they finally figure out you guys are useless out in the field so they've got you playing bellboys now? It's a good thing the mummies and daddies can be called in to fix your mess."

"We're on call for something bigger, genius," Sky had snarled, "though you wouldn't know anything about that. How was Indonesia, by the way? Get a nice tan while you were cleaning up after us?"

Jacob had narrowed his eyes but didn't rise to the bait. He had made to walk away but at the last moment he had turned to Sophie and said, "Nice to see you, Griffiths."

If it hadn't been for the sly grin aimed at Sky, and the wink he gave her, the words might have actually sounded sincere.

Sophie sighed, raising the duvet all the way up to her neck. The guy was a nightmare. Everyone knew all Jacob wanted was to be an Aster. He'd already made sure he was one of the best combat Affinites on the island. Coupled with his affinity for strategy, he would surely have caught the attention of the Small Council. Sophie had no idea how high he was on the Transfer list were she or one of her brothers to die, but the idea of Jacob being at the top...

Sophie forced herself to close her eyes and think about something else. She wondered how much sleep she would get this night, knowing that in a few hours her mother would be out there somewhere so incredibly close to Gayle Mendosa, working on a plan to get the Queen here safely. And then tomorrow afternoon she herself would enter an area of the Underworld she had never ventured into before.

Everything they had to do in the next twenty-four hours was uncharted territory for all of them. With her heart pounding in her chest, Sophie doubted she would get any real sleep at all.

It was eleven p.m. in Brazil when Madeleine Mayne and Percy Kelly strode from an abandoned side road to the outskirts of the small town near the edge of the Amazon Rainforest. They had split off from the other three Ceders about two miles earlier; Rose, Katherine and Diallo would be patrolling the perimeter of the town while Madeleine and Percy had their meeting with Tomas and Cara Mendosa.

They had tested their cloaking an hour earlier in a town near New York City. Nicholas's map had shown that there was a whole cluster of Disciples there, so they opted to walk right in their midst there first, to see if any Disciples recognised them or sensed their magic.

They hadn't. So they were safe to travel to Brazil.

Madeleine had been the only person who had visited the Mendosas frequently over the last eighteen years. Percy would go back to Saluverus only four times a year with a full report on Gayle's progress. Madeleine was the one who brought any other messages from Percy or Gayle's parents to the Small Council and the other way around. Madeleine took pride in the fact that not once in all those years had she been discovered.

Madeleine and Percy opted to stand just outside of the ring of light from a street lamp on the edge of the town. Fields set aside for farming surrounded the town on three sides, and the Amazon Rainforest bordered its back. In the darkness Madeleine couldn't make out the enormous Rainforest towering above the town on the other side. She had seen it before though, in daylight, and had always thought of it as a thing of immense beauty.

Rain had started to come down.

"Do you think she's ready?" Madeleine asked as she opened up an umbrella.

The soldier beside her looked down at her. Percy Kelly was one of the few people who was taller than the Ceder of Speed. Even without heels she was taller than the average woman. Her thin stature only emphasised her height.

"For coming tomorrow?" Percy clarified her question.

Madeleine nodded.

"Of course not," he responded with characteristic bluntness. "She was supposed to have time to process the information before leaving."

"As if two more weeks would've made such a difference," Madeleine scoffed. Her dark blue eyes were focused on the single street that led from the town to where she and the soldier were waiting. Madeleine had never agreed with the decision to bring Gayle up somewhere other than Saluverus. The man beside her had been all too supportive, and Madeleine had never tried to hide what she thought of that.

"She will be all right in the end." Percy knew full well what Madeleine thought of him, and what she thought of the decision that had been made eighteen years ago. There was no love lost between the two people standing in the darkness and the rain.

"And what of her training?"

"Are you doubting my abilities?" Percy asked, a hint of anger in his voice.

"No. I'm questioning its worth. The girl never knew why she was learning it. To her it would've been all for sport—for fun."

"What are you implying?"

Madeleine didn't bother meeting his gaze. "That she would've put in more effort, if she knew that one day her life might depend on it."

"You don't need to know that to excel at something, Madeleine." He spoke her name with antipathy. "She put in the effort because she was raised to always do so. By her parents, and by me. You don't know her like I do, so I will not stand here and have you talk to me that way."

Madeleine ignored him. "And what of that bubbly, kind nature you were always so worried about?" She chuckled coldly at the small twitch in his face as he stared her down. "Oh, don't think I haven't heard of your *concerns*. She hasn't grown up with violence and *real* combat."

"Some would say that's a good thing," Percy snarled.

"Not for being our future Queen."

"Madeleine—"

She turned to the soldier and interrupted. "If this King is anything like his predecessor there will be a war. And as Queen she will have to lead it."

"She will learn to lead," Percy said firmly.

"It's not just about leading. Anyone can be taught to lead if they have to. It's about the killing. Will she be able to shut out that colourful, gentle part of herself to be able to take a Disciple's life – a King's life even – if she hasn't been prepared for it all her life?"

Percy didn't answer the question. Instead he said, "It's been eighteen years, Madeleine. It's about time you accepted the choice that was made."

Madeleine looked towards the darkened town in front of her and straightened her shoulders. Her grip tightened on her umbrella. "I will accept it once there is proof that it was in fact the right decision," she said coldly. "Gayle hasn't even left the town yet and four Affinites are dead, six are missing and an unknown King is on the loose." She dropped her voice and muttered, "I don't like it. I don't trust it."

"You're forgetting the eighteen years where they have lived in peace, exactly what they made the decision for. You're choosing to ignore how well it has worked so far," Percy said.

Madeleine squinted, and made out a black car turning the corner onto the road that led out of the town. Madeleine and Percy moved forward into the light of the street lamp. The car stopped, and two figures stepped out on either side.

"It's never about how long it's gone right," Madeleine said as Cara and Tomas Mendosa walked towards them. "All everyone will remember, is that one moment when it all went wrong."

None of the Asters had expected to be standing in the Board Room in the middle of the night because of a summoning again. It had been the second time in three nights, and even though Sky understood there would be an urgency to it, he couldn't help getting annoyed that again he wouldn't be able to get a good night's sleep.

Less than five minutes had passed between jumping out of bed and shimmering himself and his siblings to the Board Room. Axel Reed was there waiting for them, together with Jackson Kelly and Nicholas Nelson.

For a moment Sky thought about asking Jackson what he had learnt from the Disciple he had been interrogating, but kept his mouth shut, knowing that now wasn't the time for asking questions. Now was the time to strap on weapons and hear about what the hell had gone wrong.

When Sky had woken, he'd had just enough time to check his bedside alarm clock to know that his mother and the other Ceders were already in Brazil somewhere, discussing plans with Tomas and Cara Mendosa. He desperately hoped their summoning was not related to the Ceders' mission; from the tension in his siblings he could tell they were preparing themselves for the possibility of that news, too.

"Your parents are in Gayle's town as we speak," Axel said as the Asters strapped on their weapons that had been laid out on the oak table once again. "But this is about something else." There was a collective relaxing of the tension in the Asters' bearings. "Just like with the Okoth family, we have received an emergency signal from Eileen Stewart. We don't know what about; we only have the signal. You must go now."

And immediately the tension was back. Sky tried, just like his siblings, not to stare at Matu. Josephine was Eileen Stewart's daughter. Sky glanced at Matu momentarily. His brother was methodically strapping on his knuckle knives as if it was any other mission, but Sky saw that Matu's eyes were distant. His mind would be racing. They all knew what had happened to the other Affinites that were attacked. The odds were slim that they would go to Canada and find both Eileen and her daughter alive and well.

Sophie gently laid a hand on Matu's shoulder. "Matu?"

Matu looked up at her. "I'm fine," he replied gruffly.

It didn't sound convincing, but there was no way they could leave him behind. Sky just hoped that his brother could keep it together while they dealt with whatever was happening at the Stewart house. Sky wasn't completely sure Matu would be able to. Matu was always calm and rational; able to focus solely on the mission at hand. He had been fine when they were in the Okoth's house, and Reth Okoth was like a second father to him and Yaro like a little brother. But this was even more personal. This involved the girl he loved.

Sky didn't need Axel to have the map on the television screen zoom in to the little town in Canada, to know where to shimmer to. He'd been to Josephine's house on multiple occasions.

After checking with Matu, Sophie had turned to Axel. "An emergency at the same time as our parents' meeting with the Mendosas? I don't like this at all."

"It could be a coincidence. We hadn't expected the attacks to stop until Gayle was here," Lian said, trying to sound reassuring.

Axel said nothing, his expression deliberately neutral.

"I hate coincidences," Sky muttered.

"Go now," Axel commanded, when they had finished strapping on their weapons.

The Asters clustered together in a circle, each holding on to the person standing on either side of them. Sky placed his hands on Lian and Nathan's shoulders and shimmered the five of them to the Stewart's house in Canada.

When the blue light vanished from his vision, Sky had expected the house to be in darkness. He had shimmered them right in to the kitchen, and even though he wasn't always sure of his time zones, he had expected it to be dark both inside and out, with the wires cut. It was dark outside, but the lights were on.

Sky had to blink a few times before he could take in the scene. The place didn't look as bad as the other three homes had done. Sure, a few cupboards had been opened and their contents had been thrown out over the floor. But none of the doors of the kitchen cupboards had been pulled off their hinges and the drawers from a big dresser hadn't been tossed across the room.

"Over here," came a voice from the next room.

Sky and the others hurried into the living-dining room. Here, too, all the lights were on and the furniture seemed pretty much intact. The table hadn't been thrown on its side and all the chairs were still standing.

Even Eileen Stewart seemed to be in better shape than all the other

Affinites they had encountered recently. Granted, she was alive, but she also looked a whole lot better than Eidi Okoth had done, who had only survived the Disciple attack by a stroke of luck.

Eileen was sitting on the floor with her back against one of the two sofas in the living room. Her face was swollen and bruised and there were a few cuts up and down her arms. But her chest and abdomen seemed to be untouched.

Her legs, however, were a different story. Her right leg was lying at an odd angle, with a bone near her ankle sticking out. And her left knee looked absolutely horrible.

Sophie dropped to her knees immediately and covered the woman's ankle with her right hand to start the healing. "What happened?" she asked.

"Disciples came, like the others…" Eileen began, but Matu interrupted her impatiently.

"Where's Josie?" he demanded.

Eileen looked up at the boy who had been in a relationship with her daughter for the past two years. She cast her eyes down and shook her head.

"NO!" Matu yelled. He turned away from the woman on the floor, his hands clutching his head, his eyes closed.

Sky watched Sophie as her Band glowed golden and the bone near Eileen's ankle vanished under a fresh new layer of skin. He then turned to Nathan and Lian. "Check upstairs."

The two boys nodded and were about to head out of the living room when Eileen stopped them. "Don't bother."

Sky frowned. "What are you talking about? What exactly happened here?"

Sophie didn't need to move her glowing hand over the rest of Eileen's body for all the other injuries to heal. While she kept her hand on Eileen's ankle, Sky saw the insides of her smashed knee move and knit together, until eventually the skin closed over the top and nothing was left of the injury. Behind him, Matu was muttering something under his breath. Sky couldn't understand what he was saying, which made Sky extremely worried. Matu wouldn't start muttering in Swahili unless he was close to losing control over his emotions.

Nathan was watching Matu with narrowed eyes, too, probably judging whether Matu would manage to pull it together. It was Lian who placed a hand on Matu's shoulder. Sky saw Matu was about to shrug it off, but he closed his eyes instead, and took a deep breath.

Sophie cleared her throat. She had finished healing Eileen, and besides her ankle and knee, the Affinite's face was also as good as new; the swelling had gone down completely and the bruises and shallow cuts had vanished, too.

"They came for me." Eileen pushed herself up onto the sofa. "They thought I might know Gayle's location."

"Were they wearing brown leather with red lining?" Sophie asked.

"Yes. They came with double-bladed axes."

Well, that confirmed what they already knew. All the Disciples taking Affinites were serving the same King. The same damn King the Asters knew nothing about.

"I couldn't tell them what they wanted to know. They brought Josie down. They thought that, with the right *encouragement*, I would suddenly remember Gayle's location." At this Matu hissed some more Swahili under his breath. Eileen spoke quickly and clearly. She had been trained to do so. She was talking about the infliction of violence upon her daughter, yet she spoke as if she was narrating a sports event. It was almost chilling to hear her speak so easily. "But as they were getting her, I managed to send the signal. They found out, and they vanished with her before you could come."

Matu was still turned away from Eileen. The distance in his eyes was gone now. There was a focus on his face, and Sky noticed that his hands were clenched into fists at his side. His brother was squeezing them so tightly that his knuckles were turning white.

"How did they manage to get out so quickly?" Sky asked.

"They flashed out of here in a bolt of lightning."

Matu turned back at that. "Lightning?"

"Astaroth's magic..." Sophie said. "He transported with lightning."

"We never knew he could transport others from this distance," Lian said.

"Well, now we do," Sky snapped. It explained how this King's Disciples were able to pop up and attack any Affinite house in the world, and be gone seconds later. How the Asters had always been too late.

"You should've come to Saluverus," Matu said accusingly.

Eileen looked up at Matu. As she was sitting on the sofa, Matu towered over her. She didn't seem to resent his anger. There was a sadness in her eyes. Matu was probably the only one in the room who understood what losing Josephine meant to her. "We were planning on traveling to Whitehorse early in the morning after we finished packing everything up here. I couldn't have Disciples going through classified information while we were away. We knew this could happen."

"You should've come faster," Matu growled.

"You're not hearing me," Eileen told Matu through clenched teeth. "I said *we knew this could happen.*"

Matu frowned at the woman sitting on the sofa in front of him.

"Get the box out of the bottom left drawer."

Matu did as asked and returned with a small hard-sided package in his hand.

"Open it."

Matu did so again, and pulled out a small square device with a screen on the front and an antenna sticking out of the top. There was a little strip of space left at the bottom of the screen for a few buttons.

Matu breathed in sharply and closed his eyes. "Is this what I think it is?" he asked ever so calmly.

Sky looked from the device in Matu's hand to Eileen. He didn't want to get his hopes up, but...

"I knew the Small Council was working on a technology to track Affinite essence in the Underworld. But I needed my own failsafe if we were going to stay here a while longer and risk getting attacked." Eileen pointed at the screen. "It's connected to a transmission chip I placed in Josie's arm yesterday. If you're right, then this won't just take you to my daughter. It will take you to all of the other abducted Affinites, too."

Sky stared at the woman in front of him. She was such an unpretentious woman. She was short and skinny, with lifeless blonde hair that was already streaked with grey. And yet she was one of the highest-ranking Watchers, knowing what she did about the Small Councils plans and developments. How she'd managed to get her hands on a tracker and transmission chip, like each of the Asters had in their arm, was anybody's guess. But Sky didn't care. In fact, he found her utterly remarkable; she had just given them the only lead they had to all the Affinites in the Underworld. Then something struck him...

It struck Matu a second sooner. "You didn't just stay behind to pack all your things, did you?" *You lured them here on purpose so we could get a location in the Underworld.* The unspoken words hung in the air. Sky could barely believe it. That she would use her own daughter to help the Small Council and the Asters. Her own daughter...

"Are you out of your DAMN mind?" Matu shouted. With the tracker still in his left hand, his Band blazed bronze as he flung the tracker's packaging in his right hand across the room. With the magic he had subconsciously called up, when the packaging hit a large picture hanging on the wall, the glass of the painting shattered and fell to the ground, leaving the frame hanging askew. Matu advanced on Eileen. He towered over her as he shouted, "This is Josie! How could you do that to your own daughter! You should have kept her safe!"

Lian came forward. He placed his hands on his brother's chest and gently pushed him back. "Easy…"

Matu let himself get pushed back, but the anger hadn't left him. Instead another flood of Swahili words came out of his mouth as he turned away from Eileen and covered his face with his hands.

Sky turned to Eileen and found the woman looking straight at him. Matu's outburst hadn't fazed her one bit. There was a coldness in her eyes. Sky could only stare at her silently, shocked at what she had done.

"Call your Ambassador and give him the update," the woman said. "Then use that tracker and go get my daughter back."

Chapter 12

Madeleine Mayne watched the black car vanish back around the corner and into the town. The meeting had gone better than she had expected. Both Tomas and Cara understood the necessity of getting Gayle behind Saluverus' Curtain as quickly as possible. Not just for the Queen's safety, but also for the safety of all the Affinites around the world.

With one hand on her umbrella, Madeleine used her other hand to fish her phone from her pocket and start dialling. The rain was coming down harder now. Thunder rumbled in the distance. Aside from the single street lamp above their heads there was no other light illuminating the space around her and Percy. Madeleine would've liked to use her shimmering magic to conjure up some of that blue light on the spot, but her magic could be tracked, and they needed to remain undetected until the future Queen was safely on Saluverus.

Percy Kelly remained silent beside her as Axel answered after the first ring.

"Madeleine," the Ambassador said by way of greeting.

Madeleine didn't bother with any formalities either and got straight to the point. "The meeting went well. The trip will happen exactly like we planned it. Cara and Tomas are not happy about the timing, but they understand the necessity. They are on their way back now to tell Gayle everything. She will have the rest of the night and the morning to process it before she leaves."

"Good. The perimeter was clear?"

"Yes. No Disciples around."

She knew this, because, as Cara and Tomas were walking away, she'd sent messages to the three other Ceders to come back to the meeting point. They had all responded with the same piece of information: they had detected nothing.

"Check it one more time and prepare the place we discussed for transportation. Check the air routes again. I want nothing going wrong tomorrow, Madeleine."

"We'll make sure of it." Madeleine could hear the tension in the Ambassador's voice. She pulled her phone away from her ear and ended the call. When she looked up, she saw Matu's father, Diallo, appear from around the left corner of the town. Madeleine looked to her right and saw Nathan's mother, Rose, and Katherine Griffiths walking towards her, too. The three of them had set up sensors all around the town. Those sensors would send a signal if any dark energy went past them into the town.

Madeleine turned her attention to the empty street in front of her. She hadn't realised how long she had been staring until Percy cleared his throat.

"What is it?" he asked. She must have had a look on her face that revealed what she was feeling. She didn't trust it. None of it.

"Nothing to concern yourself with," she replied coldly.

Rose, Diallo and Katherine came up beside her. The rain was streaming down their faces. Thunder rumbled closer by. A flash of lightning lit up the sky for a brief moment. Madeleine didn't like the feel of the storm; there was something about the lightning, its energy, that she couldn't put her finger on.

"Sensors in place?" she asked.

The three Ceders nodded that all was fine.

Good. Madeleine felt herself relax marginally. With the sensors working, no dark entity, whether Disciple or King, would be able to enter the town without them knowing about it. The Mendosas were safe for now.

"We'll go back to the car and travel to the place where they will be transporting from. We need to make sure it is still secure before we go back to Saluverus," Madeleine said.

No one disagreed with her as she turned her back on the town and headed down the darkened road running between the fields.

Madeleine understood the need to travel from a different place. If the unknown King knew where the Mendosas had spent the last eighteen years of their lives, he would no doubt use the lives of the people within that town against them. It wouldn't be the first time. The location of where Gayle had lived until she was eighteen should remain secret for the rest of her life.

Madeleine strode ahead of the others towards where they had parked their car, two miles off. Rain was clattering down upon her umbrella. Madeleine would have much rather shimmered, saving her this dreadfully wet walk, but she would have to endure it to remain undetected.

Lightning flashed brightly over their heads, shortly followed by a clap of thunder. The storm had moved to right above them.

Madeleine glanced up at the sky. Even though the meeting had gone well and everything was going to plan, there was a new sort of tension in her body that she couldn't shake off. There didn't seem to be any reason to feel that way, but she couldn't help the bad feeling from spreading through her body as she, the other Ceders and Percy walked further and further away from their future Queen.

Unfortunately, Sky couldn't shimmer straight to Josephine. He couldn't shimmer into the Underworld unless he had been to that specific place before. What also delayed them was that because Josephine was somewhere underground, the signal coming from the tracking chip in her arm was slightly erratic. The odds that Sky would be able to shimmer them very close to where she was, but on the Surface, were slim. All Sky could do was focus on the inconsistent signal from the tracker and see how close he could get.

Nathan could feel the tension in Sky's grip on his shoulder as he shimmered. Blue light filled Nathan's vision and for a moment it felt like he was floating in space. The second the blue light vanished the Asters were enveloped in darkness and rain was crashing down on top of them.

Nathan's magic almost sizzled in his veins as it recognised where it was. Nathan knew instinctively that they were in the Amazon Rainforest, a place he had always dreamed of visiting; but that dream felt more like a distant spark as the cold mission state settled over him. He crouched down and placed his hands on the muddy ground. His Band glowed brightly as his magic rushed through his body towards his hands and into the ground. He could detect an Underworld tunnel right beneath them. Nathan closed his eyes, shut out the hammering of the rain and focused on his magic. Seconds later, mere inches away from his fingers, the ground started to open up. Nathan willed the earth to morph into what he needed it to become. It was barely visible in the darkness, but a long stretch of steps had materialised, leading right down into the South American Underworld.

"It's done! Go!" Nathan shouted at the others through the rain. His siblings rushed past him and ran down the stairs. Matu was first, clutching the tracker in one hand and a torch in the other. Once all four of them had gone ahead, Nathan followed. As he ran down, he traced his fingers along the earth on both sides. His Band glowed again, and the earth closed above his head, and with every step he went down, the steps behind him were once again replaced with dense earth.

The steps seemed to go on forever. Deeper and deeper the Asters raced down into the depths of the earth, until finally the light from Matu's torch no longer pointed downwards, but straight ahead. When Nathan joined them on the tunnel floor, the opening to the steps closed up completely behind him. They only stood in the torchlight for a moment. Lanterns all along the walls flashed on in a burst of magical fire, and suddenly the Asters were standing in the light.

Nathan looked around. Even those few minutes outside had been enough to completely soak them to the skin. Matu was staring at the tracker in his hands. Sophie peered around him to look at the screen as well.

"The signal's strong down here. We don't seem to be too far away," Sophie said.

"You're welcome," Sky preened.

Sophie looked up from the tracker. "Now is not the time, and you know it."

Sky huffed, but kept grinning to himself nonetheless.

"Any idea what district we're in?" Lian asked, changing the subject.

Each Underworld territory was divided up into districts, interconnected open caverns that held not only living quarters like houses, mansions and even castles, but also industrial complexes for producing foods and goods. Nathan remembered something about underground rivers being harnessed to provide electricity. The districts were connected to each other by a vast network of tunnels, some of them hundreds of miles long.

Nathan looked in both directions of the tunnel they were in, but found that both looked completely identical. The tunnels connecting the different districts usually did. This one was about twenty five feet wide and well-lit. Nathan would bet that they were near one of the larger districts.

"Impossible to tell from here," Sophie said. "Once we get to a cavern I might be able to tell."

"It doesn't matter where we are," Matu said impatiently. "Come on."

With the tracker raised in front of him, he headed down the tunnel to Nathan's right at a run. The other Asters followed quickly. Sophie made sure she was running alongside Matu, glancing at the tracker every few steps, though Nathan had no doubt she would rather having the tracker in her own hands. Nathan also thought it was better for her to lead them, since she knew more about this Underworld than any of them, but they both knew that Matu would never relinquish the one thing that connected him to Josephine.

Sky and Lian followed closely behind Matu and Sophie, while Nathan brought up the rear. The tunnel they ran down stretched out in a straight line in front of them. Nathan didn't know why he had expected it to look different from the other territories, but it didn't. The floors were the same black tiles and the walls and ceiling were simply the brown colour of the soil above. The only difference to the other Underworld territories he had been in were the black and red swirling lines painted on the walls.

They ran on for what seemed like an eternity. Being all the way at the back, Nathan couldn't tell what was coming up ahead, and whether they were reaching the end of the tunnel.

No sooner had he thought that than Lian and Sky stopped running, and Nathan skidded to a halt to avoid crashing into them. In front of him, Sophie and Matu stepped forward and to their right, out of sight.

Sky and Lian followed. Nathan could hear Matu swear under his breath and Lian gasp. It was only when Sky and Lian moved out of the way, and Nathan could step forward, that he saw where they had arrived.

The five of them were standing on a small rectangular slab of rock, near the top of an enormous cavern. On the right hand side of the platform was a staircase that led all the way down to the floor a hundred yards below them. Neither the landing they were standing on, nor the stairs leading down, had bannisters.

Nathan looked around the cavern, silently taking in the remarkable space. There were hundreds of tunnel openings at different heights in the cavern walls. All those above ground level had an open staircase, just like the one that the Asters were standing on, leading down to the ground. A narrow but rushing river cut through the cavern in the middle. On the opposite side of the river to where the Asters were standing, was a tunnel opening different to every other one in the cavern. This tunnel entrance was taller and grander than any of the others. For starters, this one had a double door. It was at least ten feet tall and symbols of fire and lightning, decorated in colours of red, black and silver, had been carved into the walls around it. The two halves of the double door looked like thick tubes of steel woven together like a fishing net.

Matu started the descent down to the cavern floor, moving more slowly now than he had done in the tunnel. Even in his rush to save Josephine, he was smart enough to know that one wrong step would have him falling headfirst into a hundred yard drop.

"That's the entrance to the Sera," Sophie breathed.

Nathan had heard of that name before...

"English please," Sky said impatiently from behind her.

"It's also called the Lock," Sophie explained as the five of them hurried down the steps. Nathan suddenly realised where they were. He looked up and stared at the Lock's entrance once again. "It's the one and only entrance to what was Astaroth's capital district. No Merger has ever been able to get inside. Only Aiyana has ever been there."

In front of Nathan, Lian let out a low whistle.

The Sera explained why the Mergers in this Underworld had not managed to find out that the abducted Affinites were in this territory all along, and why, all this time, they had never found out who the new King was and how he worked. If the King had spent all of the last twenty-five years in the Sera, biding his time, calculating and planning, no wonder the Asters had been one step behind every time he'd made a move.

Then something struck Nathan. The entire cavern was completely empty. There was not a single Disciple to be seen; not going in or out of any of the hundreds of tunnels that led to the cavern, nor up or down any of the staircases, nor crossing the river or the cavern floor. And what was even more worrying, the double steel-woven doors were standing wide open. No Disciple guards were posted on the outside. It was as if the King was welcoming them inside a place that no Merger or Aster had ever even been able to fight their way into. As if he had been expecting them all along.

Once at the bottom of the stairs, the Asters ran along the open, barren ground. Further up and down from them were bridges over the river, but without breaking stride the Asters took the direct route across. The river was narrow enough that none of them had any trouble jumping over it to the other side.

As they neared the entrance to the Sera, Matu said, "Prepare yourself. We might meet resistance soon."

"Doesn't look like they're being very resistant so far," Sky said.

"No doubt it's a trap," Sophie said from up ahead, putting into words what they had all already concluded.

"It doesn't matter," Matu growled. And he was right. It didn't matter. They needed to find the abducted Affinites and get them out safely before Gayle Mendosa travelled to Saluverus. They had expected this mission to start tomorrow afternoon, after Glacialis' tracking system had been finished. At least now they had an extra ten hours to work with.

Nathan flexed his hands. He was ready to reach for one of the broadswords strapped to his back if he needed to. Even though everything seemed quiet, he knew that it wouldn't last. The King wouldn't just let them rescue the Affinites without a fight.

But then why weren't they being followed? Nathan was dead certain that they had been detected by now. Their mere presence would set off detection sensors all over the place. The Asters hadn't even bothered to use cloaking spells. They wouldn't be very effective anyway; dark magic clung to the walls and ground like it was a living organism. Aster magic was too stark a contrast to the dark energy moving all around them to go unnoticed.

And it was that same dark energy that Nathan could practically feel against his skin. It got stronger the closer they got to the doors.

Nathan cast one last look over his shoulder before following his siblings through the open steel-woven doors and into the Sera. Once again he couldn't see any Disciple coming through any of the tunnels. It didn't feel right. None of it did.

In fact, something felt very, very wrong.

It had been half an hour since Madeleine Mayne's phone call, and Axel was the only one still in the Board Room. He was sitting at the corner desk, looking up something on the computer. He had changed the settings on the television: it no longer showed a map of the world, but instead the images of the six Ceders. Rose, Katherine and Madeleine made up the top three images, while Diallo, Cara and Tomas made up the bottom three.

Despite having moved away from Saluverus eighteen years ago, Tomas and Cara still had their transmitting chips in their upper right arms. The chips still sent in their vitals whenever Axel pulled them up onto the screen. Considering their plan to travel with Gayle to the island tomorrow, Axel considered it essential to have their information right in front of him, too.

Axel finished typing on the keyboard and the second computer screen lit up, showing the five images of the Asters. Even though the meeting with the Mendosas had been of primary importance, Axel certainly hadn't forgotten that the Asters were on a mission of their own.

Eileen Stewart had been smart, though Axel was still adamant to call it reckless. She had put her only child's life in immense danger to get the Asters and the Small Council the information and the opportunity they needed to get the abducted Affinites out of the South American Underworld. Eileen had known that her daughter would remain alive, at least for a while, but that still didn't give her the right to risk Josephine's life. Axel didn't even know if Josephine had agreed to it. Axel already had a plan to suspend Eileen from her Watcher duties, until he was sure that she would not do something like this again.

Axel looked at the computer. The Asters were doing fine. If the lighting of an image got darker, or started flickering, it meant that that Aster was in trouble. If the entire picture went dark, it meant that the chip couldn't pick up any vital signs anymore. If that happened, then the Aster was dead.

Axel still believed they should've given Gayle Mendosa a chip of her own years ago so that her well-being could be monitored as well. Her parents had refused at the time, believing that she would be safe in that town. And she had been. But even they knew they couldn't take any chances in the next forty-eight hours. Madeleine had been given a small briefcase with everything the Mendosas would need to implant the chip into Gayle's arm tonight. Just so that if anything were to go wrong in the next few days, the Small Council would know exactly where their future Queen was.

The Ambassador sighed and stared at the screens. He didn't know how long he sat there until he decided he needed to stretch his legs. But he had barely made it out of his chair when suddenly two images on the television screen started flickering and an alarm went off.

Axel jumped and stared up at the screen. It was Cara and Tomas Mendosa. Both of their images were darkening and flickering wildly.

Then from one moment to the next, their images went completely dark.

"WHAT?" Madeleine screamed into her phone. She could barely understand the frantic words coming out of the Ambassador's mouth, except for one thing: Tomas and Cara's vital signs were gone. Their images were dark.

"Turn back now! See what is going on NOW!" Axel thundered through the phone.

They were almost at their car, two miles from the town, and Madeleine wasn't going to waste any time by running back. She didn't give the others any sort of warning when she threw down her umbrella, reached out and grabbed Rose and Diallo's wrists and yelled, "Hold on!"

Percy and Katherine only had seconds to understand what Madeleine was about to do before she shimmered, but they were already on high alert from her response to Axel's phone call; they reacted instinctively to her tone and command, and immediately grasped Rose and Diallo's free hands.

The five of them re-appeared right where Madeleine and Percy had met the Mendosas only half an hour earlier. "Did the sensors pick anything up?" Madeleine yelled through the rain. It was still hammering down, and Madeleine could barely see her companions through the downpour.

Rose, Katherine and Diallo all shook their heads.

"What's going on?" Percy shouted through the rain.

"Cara and Tomas are dead!" Madeleine called over her shoulder. She was already heading for the street that led into the town, when suddenly she crashed up against an invisible wall.

"What the hell," she growled, and pushed again. There was definitely something blocking her path towards the town, but there was nothing visible in front of her.

The three Ceders and Percy Kelly came up beside her. "And Gayle?" Percy shouted.

"Axel doesn't know! They hadn't implanted the chip yet!" Madeleine threw her shoulder against the invisible barrier, but it didn't give an inch. "I can't get through!"

"Move!" Diallo came up beside her and pulled his arm back. The Band on his wrist glowed a deep bronze as he used his magic of Strength. His fist landed against something physical, and black lines rippled from where his hand met the invisible wall. The barrier, however, didn't break.

"It's a dark veil! I need more power!"

The three women immediately knew what to do. They gathered around Diallo. Madeleine stood right behind him and held out her hands to Katherine and Rose, who stood on either side of her. Katherine, to her left, took Madeleine's left hand with her right, and she placed her own left hand on Diallo's shoulder. Rose did the exact opposite on Madeleine's right. The moment the circle was whole, the three women started whispering a spell under their breath; a spell for Diallo to be able to use the power of their magic to make his stronger.

Madeleine could hardly hear Rose and Katherine's chanting through the pouring rain. The Bands on their wrists started glowing and Diallo pulled his arm back. With lightning speed he threw it forward. Darkness rippled from where his fist hit the barrier. But this time the darkness didn't disappear entirely like the first time. Dark cracks in the otherwise invisible shield remained.

"Again!" Madeleine commanded.

The three women started chanting again. Their Bands shone brightly in the darkness and through the rain.

Diallo punched the wall again. Darkness rippled, and the cracks grew larger.

"Again!" Diallo shouted.

And they did.

After Diallo's third punch there were not only cracks, but large ridges that Madeleine could see through. She didn't have to say anything as the women beside her started chanting again.

Madeleine hissed the words through her teeth, trying to control the fear and anger building up inside of her. How had they been so stupid? Though they had no reason to believe that the unknown King of the South American Underworld knew of Gayle's location, they hadn't thought of the possibility of a dark entity already being so close. That must have been why the sensors didn't pick up any Dark magic heading into the town: they were already inside. And they had put up this dark veil *after* the Mendosas had driven back across the border of the town, locking themselves in, and keeping everyone else out.

Diallo rallied another punch, and this time the darkness rippled even thicker and further than before. Then, without any warning, the darkness flashed a bright, deep red and vanished.

Madeleine didn't wait around. She dug into her magic and flew down the street. The town wasn't large; she would be in the main street in seconds. At the first T- junction she turned right. At the next small intersection she turned left.

At that point she was hovering in the main street and couldn't believe what she was seeing.

It was completely empty. There were no Disciples anywhere to be seen. Madeleine shot up into the sky and scanned the streets below. There was no movement anywhere. She caught sight of a group of people running, but realised quickly that they were her fellow Ceders and Percy Kelly.

Madeleine didn't fly over to meet them. Instead she swooped to the ground and took a sharp turn to the right. She knew where the Mendosas lived: they had a two-story house up against a small hill just off the main street.

With all her magic of Speed and Flight, Madeleine flew towards the Mendosas' house. As it loomed up above her, she saw that Tomas and Cara's car wasn't there, and that the front door had been completely broken down and was lying face down in the hallway beyond. Without a second's thought, Madeleine flew inside and flashed through every room of the house. There was no one in the kitchen, or the living-dining space. Madeleine barely registered how the place had been completely trashed. She only cared about one thing: where was Gayle Mendosa?

Madeleine shot up to the small space under the roof and into the tiny second bedroom up there. Gayle wasn't there. The bedroom was completely empty. Madeleine didn't bother going back out through the main door. She noticed that the bedroom window had been smashed, and she flew straight through it. Madeleine gave herself a few seconds to see if there was any way down from that window, and felt relief flood through her momentarily when she spotted the drainpipe.

The broken window... and the drain pipe... Gayle might have been able to run.

Madeleine flew down and back to the main street and found Rose, Katherine, Diallo and Percy standing there, wide-eyed in horror. It was only then that Madeleine registered the destruction of the main street. It was like a gigantic knife had been pulled right down the middle of it.

Madeleine hung above it for a second and realised that what she thought was a chasm, was actually only a few feet deep. She didn't understand the significance of it, and therefore didn't care. She dropped to the ground and reached for something in her jacket pocket.

"The house?" Percy shouted through the downpour. His dark hair was plastered to the sides of his face.

"Empty! But she might've got away!"

Madeleine found what she was looking for in her pocket and revealed it. The other Ceders stared at the small vial in her hands. Tomas Mendosa had given it to her during their meeting less than an hour earlier. The vial contained Gayle Mendosa's blood.

"If anything should go wrong, use it. If, for some reason, that chip doesn't work, this will be the only way you'll be able to find her," Tomas had said.

Madeleine now bent over the vial, as if to shield it from the clattering rain, and emptied half of its content onto the palm of her hand. Percy took the vial from her, so that Madeleine could close her other hand on top of the one holding Gayle's blood.

With her fingers intertwined, and Gayle's blood oozing through her fingers, Madeleine held her hands to her mouth and whispered the words of a tracking spell. All eyes were on her, and Madeleine saw the growing awareness in each of them as they realised the worst might have happened right under their noses.

Madeleine closed her eyes and focused on finishing the tracking spell perfectly. She could feel the blood warm in her hands; her heart hammering in her chest. There was only a light tingling across her palms and the inside of her fingers – usually a tracking spell would also tug her hands into a particular direction – but it was enough to tell her that Gayle was still alive.

But something was blocking her spell. Or *someone*.

Gayle was alive, but she was still actively being hunted, and Madeleine knew they wouldn't have a lot of time. If they were going to break through whatever was blocking her spell, Madeleine would need more Aster power than that of one generation. If she could get a precise location by using a lot more power, she could shimmer right to where Gayle was, blockage or not.

"Hold on!" Madeleine commanded again.

All the Ceders and Percy Kelly did as they were told, and Madeleine shimmered them all out of the town.

A second later the four of them, completely drenched to the skin, appeared in the Board Room. At the desk, Axel shot up from his chair, eyes glaring.

"WHAT ARE YOU—" he started, but Madeleine wouldn't let him finish.

"Get me the Asters!" she shouted at the Ambassador.

Axel's face whitened slightly. "They are in the South American Underworld getting the Affinites out."

Madeleine couldn't spare even one second to panic. If she couldn't use the younger, current generation of Aster magic to make her spell strong enough to find Gayle... then she would need the older generation instead.

"Get me a bag of salt, a candle and some matches while I go and get the Elders; we don't have much time! She won't be alive for long!"

Chapter 13

After only about half a mile inside the Sera, the Asters had made a turn that led them down a set of steps and further into the depths of the South American Underworld. At the bottom, they found themselves once again running through a series of tunnels.

Matu's eyes were glued to the tracker as he made each turn. He could see the orange dot on the screen, and he could see the path towards it. The technology was simple, but it worked. It didn't give him any information about what state Josie would be in once they found her, but at this point he only cared about finding her.

He still couldn't believe that it was Josie he was tracking. That Eileen had risked her own daughter's life so that the Asters had a lead and could find the other Affinites in the Underworld.

Her own daughter.

It was as if Eileen knew for sure that Josephine would live through this. That her daughter would be fine. But Matu had heard the stories, and he knew for a fact that Eileen had heard them as well. From Eidi Okoth they had learnt that even the children weren't safe. Yaro had been hit right in front of Eidi and Reth to try and get them to talk. What the hell had been going through Eileen's mind to even think about putting her daughter through that?

That Eileen was committed to her job as a Watcher was not in doubt. What Matu did doubt was if she was as good at her job of being a mother.

He'd heard enough from Josephine to suspect that she wasn't.

Matu reached the end of another corridor. He was about to dash to his left, but Sophie stopped him, like she'd done at every other intersection they'd come across. Matu waited for Sophie to look in both directions and listen intently for a moment. The second she nodded that the coast was clear Matu raced on.

He knew he wasn't at his sharpest. How could he be? When the life of the girl he loved was at stake? But some part of him wasn't worried that he wasn't at his best. He had complete faith in the people behind him. Every single corridor they had run through up until now looked the same to him, but he knew Sophie would be paying attention and know the way back. He also knew Sky was ready to shimmer them out if they really ran into trouble. And that Nathan would be the first to know whether trouble would arrive: at regular intervals, Nathan would touch the wall with his right hand and magically grow a tiny root there that could communicate with him. Matu knew the roots couldn't exactly *speak* to Nathan, but if the dark energy of a Disciple passed it, indicating that they were being followed, Nathan would be the first to know.

The orange dot on the screen was getting closer. Matu tried not to think about how lucky they had been not to run into any Disciples yet. He also tried not to think about the fact that it probably had nothing to do with luck. He just hoped that there wouldn't suddenly be an entire army coming after them all at once, or waiting for them at the prison cells. Even so, they were prepared for those scenarios as well.

They turned another corner. Matu had only moments to take in a huge painting of two lightning bolts crossing each other, before they moved on. He hated that symbol; Astaroth's symbol. There had never been another King with his kind of magic. He had been one of the original seven. Matu remembered that the North American King was into the fifth reincarnation already. That King had never really been taken seriously. No King compared to Astaroth. Not even Kirnon, Astaroth's older brother, and the only Original King left. Even though a King became more powerful the older he became, all the terrifying stories had been about Astaroth, never Kirnon.

Matu arrived at another intersection and Sophie suddenly made him stop. Sky, Lian and Nathan pressed in against them and waited. Sophie held her hand up so they would remain still and peered around the corner. She then suddenly whipped her head back and pressed a finger to her lips. There was the sound of running footsteps, and then there were about ten Disciples running through the corridor alongside the one the Asters were in. Matu hadn't realised there was a corridor right beside their own, and that they had reached an intersection where you could turn back into the other one if you wanted.

The sound of the Disciples should've spiked fear through Matu, but instead he felt relieved that they were still around. Having such a famous district like the Sera be completely abandoned was in some ways more terrifying than having it crawling with Disciples.

Once the Disciples' footsteps echoed in the distance Sophie looked at the tracker in Matu's hand and made a U-turn into the other corridor, and headed in the direction the ten Disciples had just come from.

Matu looked down at the tracker as he followed Sophie. "We're almost there," he told the boys behind him. He couldn't believe he was so close to reaching Josie. His stunning girl, with the locks of blonde hair and the brilliant smile that could light up a whole room. Matu snarled at the thought of someone laying a hand on that beautiful face.

They came to a stop at the end of another corridor. Matu turned the corner and saw that the adjacent corridor was only about a hundred feet long with a wooden door at the end. Matu glanced down at the tracker. The orange dot was right on the other side of that door. His heart started hammering in his chest.

"She's right behind there," he said, relief in his voice.

He stepped into the corridor; it was wide enough for Sophie and

Nathan to come up on either side of him. Matu glanced sideways at his brother. There was something like suspicion in Nathan's eyes as he scanned the walls and ceiling, the Band on his wrist glowing green. Matu ignored it, and he started to quicken his pace, his eyes on the tracker, knowing that Josie was so close.

"GET BACK!" Nathan shouted. Suddenly there was an arm flung across Matu's chest and he was being thrown backwards. He landed painfully on his back, dropping the tracker in the process. Nathan was half on top of him. Matu glanced up at the door and moments later it was blown to pieces.

Matu threw up his hands and turned his head away to avoid getting hit in the face by debris, but it never came. There was a ringing in his ears from the loud bang when the door exploded. He had seen the pieces of wood flying in his direction, but they hadn't hit him.

He opened his eyes. Nathan was sitting on his knees next to him. His right hand was up in the air and the Band on his wrist was glowing a fierce green colour. Between them and the exploded door was an entire wall of brown roots, protecting them from the blast.

Matu opened his mouth to speak, but right at that moment there was a loud tearing sound. He looked up and saw that a huge crack was spreading out on the ceiling. Small pieces of rock were already raining down.

Matu scrambled to his feet. Sophie, Lian and Sky were already doing the same thing behind him.

"Nate!" he called to his brother.

Nathan turned around and followed Matu's eyes to the ceiling. He threw his hand up, Band glowing, and brown roots started stretching across the ceiling, covering the crack and holding it together.

Nathan jumped to his feet and dashed past Matu towards the other Asters, but Matu didn't move away. He stared back at the root wall that had saved them from the blast. Josie was behind there. He couldn't just run in the opposite direction.

"Matu!" Sophie came back up beside him, picked up the tracker he had dropped in his fall, and tugged on his arm. "The ceiling won't hold for long. We need to go."

Matu angrily pulled his arm back. "Josie's behind there! Right there! Nate, get rid of that wall, this will be faster!"

"There's another way to get there," Sophie reassured him urgently, looking down at the tracker and taking his arm again.

Matu didn't look at her. He looked past her to Nathan, pleading with his eyes not to pull him away now that he was so close. Nathan looked back at him. There was no emotion in his face. It was almost chilling how Nathan lost that kind side of himself when they were on missions. Only the cold and clinical remained; the focus on what they had to do and how best to do it.

"You can't get through that way," he said calmly. "We will be buried alive if we try."

Nathan's words sunk in. The ceiling gave another groan, and more bits of debris rained down. Matu covered his head and hurried alongside Sophie over to where his three brothers were waiting for him. As he reached them he turned to Sophie.

"Find me that other way, *now*," he told her.

Sophie nodded. She turned away from him and headed back down the corridor. Matu kept close behind her, followed by the other three boys.

There was a loud rumble and crash somewhere not far behind them, and Matu knew that it was the ceiling that had fallen down. Nathan had been right. He never spoke much during missions, but when he did it always mattered and he was always right. He was running alongside Matu now. His Band was still glowing green as they followed Sophie back down the long corridor, and turned right at the end.

Nathan glanced behind him. "We're being followed."

"How far behind?" Sophie asked from up front.

Matu looked sideways as his brother thought for a moment. "Two, three minutes—tops."

That wasn't long... Matu thought, worry flaring up in his stomach. "How much further?"

Just as he asked the question a side-corridor came up on their right. Sophie turned and sprinted down it. Matu had a vague idea that they were now running back towards where Josie was. When he looked over Sophie's shoulder at the tracking device he saw that they were still quite a distance away, but at least they were heading back in the right direction.

They kept on running. No one said anything as the four boys followed Sophie down the seemingly endless hallways. Matu couldn't hear their pursuers yet, and knew that if they were coming closer Nathan would let them know. Now all he could hope for was that they wouldn't meet any others in front of them. They had a plan in place for if that happened; Matu just hoped they wouldn't have to make use of it.

Matu looked over Sophie's shoulder again and saw that they were coming very close to the orange dot that indicated Josie's location. He was dismayed to see that she seemed to be so close on the other side of the wall to his right but that there was no way to get to her quickly. Even looking forward he didn't see any entrance to his right at all.

But Sophie kept on running with such confidence, and Matu forced himself to keep his mouth shut and to have faith in his sister. He moved up alongside her, matching her stride for stride.

Then suddenly Matu spotted an opening in the right-hand wall.

"Is that..." he started.

"Yep," Sophie answered through her heavier breathing.

They neared the opening, and were about sixty feet away when the whole tunnel rumbled and the ground shook beneath their feet. Matu slowed as he neared the opening, and at that moment a mass of debris blew out from the side corridor. The force of the explosion nearly knocked him off his feet. He stumbled backwards, pressing a hand against the wall to steady himself.

"No, no, no!" he shouted.

More cracks appeared on the ceiling.

Matu jumped in front of the opening – the side corridor that was supposed to get them to Josie – and found that the explosion had completely sealed it off. Huge rocks barred the way.

"We need to keep going," Sophie urged. She set off again at a run. Matu followed her closely. She had to know another way. Sophie would find another way.

"What the hell is going on?" Sky muttered from the back.

"They're trying to bury us alive," Lian answered.

"Their timing is way off," Sky replied.

The two of them grinned at each other. Matu stopped himself from snapping at his brothers. Only those two could find a way to joke around during a mission as dangerous and important as this one.

"That's because they're not trying to kill us," Sophie said from up front.

"Well, that's good," Sky said facetiously.

Sophie glared back at him. "Those explosions cost us time."

"What are you saying?" Matu asked, coming up beside her again.

Sophie glanced sideways at him. "They're trying to stall us."

As they ran alongside each other, Matu managed to stare at his sister. "For what?"

"I don't know. But whatever it is, we're running out of time."

Matu almost let out a growl.

"They're coming closer," Nathan warned from behind them, "and there's more of them."

"I thought you said they weren't trying to kill us," Sky called to the front.

The corridor swept round to the right, and Matu used a hand on the wall to make the turn. He glanced at the device in Sophie's hands. Josie was almost perpendicular to them now, on their right. He looked up ahead, and saw an indent in the wall coming up.

The Asters skidded to a halt, and Matu realised the indent was really a huge oak door built into the wall.

"Killing us is not the main objective, for some reason," Sophie said. As she spoke Matu dug into his magic, the Band on his wrist starting to glow a deep bronze colour. "But if they can kill us while we're here... I doubt they'll pass up that chance."

"They're getting closer," Nathan called out, glancing behind him. "Two minutes max."

Sky was looking up ahead of them. He had his short spear in hand, ready to fight. "It's not them we have to worry about."

Matu caught a glimpse of Disciples running towards them from the direction Sky was looking in. There was a flash of green, and great, thick roots started to grow in between the Asters and the onrushing Disciples.

"That won't hold them for long," Nathan warned.

With his magic pulsing through his body, Matu threw his fist against the door. It swung open with a groan.

He had prepared himself for an attack on the other side, but none came. The Asters hurried inside and Sky flung the door shut behind them. Nathan threw up his hand again, Band glowing green, and more roots grew, barring the door shut from the inside.

There was a tearing sound from the other side of the door, and Matu knew that that was the sound of Nathan's magical barrier of roots on the other side of the door being ripped apart.

"How long?" Sophie asked.

"No more than five minutes," Nathan answered.

But Matu wasn't listening anymore. He stared down the long hall they'd just entered. It was lined with prison cells. Small spaces had been carved into the walls and there were metal bars enclosing the prisoners inside. The prison ceilings were extremely low. A grown man would be just about able to sit up straight in one of them without banging his head.

Matu rushed down the hallway, glancing into every prison cell as he went. He skidded to a halt when he caught sight of dark hair and dark skin. Matu dropped to his knees in front of Reth Okoth's cell. The great boulder of a man could barely fit in the dug-out space behind the bars. His shoulders were hunched and he held his head low so as not to hit the roof of the cell.

"Reth!" Matu exclaimed. He dropped to his knees.

Reth Okoth lifted his head slightly. His eyes widened as he recognised Matu on the other side of the bars. The man who was like a second father to Matu had definitely seen better days. His nose was broken and his left eye was all puffy and swollen. Relief, and something else Matu didn't recognise, filled his words when Reth said, "You're here."

"Yes, we are." Matu locked his hands around two of the prison bars. He focused on his magic of Strength. The moment his Band started glowing bronze he pulled as hard as he could. The bars snapped free so easily that Matu almost toppled backwards.

"You found Eidi?" Reth asked.

At first Matu didn't understand why there was such a defeated sadness in Reth's voice until...

"She was still alive when we found her." Matu used his magic to pull out another two bars. Reth's eyes widened and he smiled such a shocked smile that it made Matu grin. "She's on Saluverus and she's fine."

With the fourth bar pulled out there was enough space for the huge Kenyan soldier to crawl out of the prison cell. But he didn't get far. Reth tried to crawl, but he couldn't seem to put any weight on his left wrist, and only in that moment did Matu see that his right leg and right shin had been broken.

Matu leaned into the cell to try and help the man, but Reth waved him off. "Help Yaro first," he said, his breathing suddenly heavy.

"Reth..."

At that moment Sophie dropped down next to Matu. She studied Reth's wounds, her Band already glowing golden, and turned to Matu. "I have this covered. Go find her."

Matu barely gave Reth a second glance. He was on his feet and running down the hallway to find the girl he loved.

Behind him, Matu could hear banging against the main door, as Disciples tried to force their way through.

"Hold it closed! We need all the time we can get!" Matu heard Sky yell. Matu knew that Nathan would be facing the door, his magic blazing as he tried to keep the door closed for as long as it took for the other Asters to get all the Affinites out.

About halfway down the hallway the path was partly blocked with fallen rocks and debris. Matu recognised it as the place where the second explosion had happened.

"Josie!" Matu called down the hall.

"Matu?" shouted back a voice all the way at the end. Matu came to an abrupt halt in front of the fallen rocks and debris. It didn't block off the hallway completely. It reached to about his waist. Matu's magic pulsed through his body as he grabbed the biggest rocks on top and threw them behind him like they weighed nothing. He didn't bother clearing a whole path, just enough to easily climb over to the other side.

Matu scrambled through and raced all the way to the end of the hallway. He dropped to his knees in front of the final prison cell and prepared himself for what he would see.

Josephine was kneeling on the other side of the metal bars. But her face wasn't one filled with relief at her being saved. It was horror.

"What are you doing here?" she cried at him.

Matu barely registered her question. A wave of relief washed through him as he saw that she had been completely untouched. There wasn't a single bruise on her delicate face, nor a single scratch on her slender arms. Not one finger had been broken. There weren't bleeding, bald patches on her head where her light blonde hair could've been pulled out. He was so relieved that she was all right that it didn't yet register that he should be suspicious precisely *because* she was completely unharmed.

"What?" he said, smiling. Happy—he was so happy that she was all right.

"You can't be here," Josie hissed between the bars.

"What are you talking about? We've come to save you."

Out of the corner of his eye, and through the path he'd made, Matu could see the other Asters working on the metal bars of the other prisons. They were whispering spells to break them, seeing as Matu was the only one with the strength to pull them off with his bare hands. He experienced a momentary flash of discomfort at his own selfishness for putting his feelings first, but it was easily drowned out by his relief at finding Josie, at her being unharmed.

Tears started to fill Josie's pale blue eyes as she reached a hand through the bars and took Matu's hand in hers. "I know you have. They've been waiting for you."

Matu didn't waste any more time. He let go of Josie's hand and he clasped his around two of the metal bars. His Band started glowing that deep bronze again and he ripped the metal bars right out of their frame. It wasn't quite enough space for Josie to come through, so Matu focused his magic again and pulled out another two bars.

"If they've been waiting for us," Matu muttered as he helped Josie out of the prison and up onto her feet, "then why didn't they attack the second we arrived here? Why wait that long?"

Matu pulled her into an embrace. Josie hugged him tightly, but only for a second. She pulled herself away and searched Matu's face. "Because they want you here. Don't you understand? They want you *here*, so you can't be *up there*."

Matu frowned. "What are you talking about?"

They hurried back towards the other Asters. Matu helped Josie climb over the rocks still blocking part of the hallway.

"The King knows Gayle's location," Josie said as she hopped down on the other side of the debris. "Reth said so after they locked me in here."

"What?" Matu's heart pounded hard in his chest as he landed next to her. "But no Affinite here knew—"

"They already knew, Matu. They've known all this time. This, us—" Josie gestured down the hallway, where not only Yaro and Reth were out of their cells now, but also Orla Brown and her son Eli, and Amisha and Citra Jasman, too, "—it was all just to get you here."

"Can't hold for much longer!" Nathan called evenly from the door. The pounding against the wood was getting louder and Matu could see the roots stretching and the wood behind them splintering.

"It's all fine," Matu tried to speak calmly as the two of them reached the others. "Our parents are up there. They are there right now, in fact. They are strong enough to protect Gayle—"

"*Matu.* You're not hearing what Josephine is saying." The strength in Reth Okoth's voice made everyone turn around to listen to him. "They knew all of it. They've planned for it. They knew your parents would be called in, so they used *us* to get you here. Your parents won't be strong enough to protect Gayle. They've been saying as much for days now; they've been gloating."

"They? Not *him*?" Sophie asked. "You've not seen the King?"

"It's only been Disciples down here," Reth said. Yaro was pressed tightly against his father's side. The young boy nodded in agreement with his father.

"But they've known all of it," Josie said desperately. "You need to get back. Your parents won't be enough. They've known Gayle's location from the start. Don't you see? We're just a distraction!"

"Guys!" Nathan called with unusual urgency. Wood splintered and snapped.

Sky wasted no time. "Everybody in a circle! Hold on to the people each side of you, NOW!"

There was a ringing in Matu's ears as everything that had happened, and what he had heard, fell into place. He barely registered the Affinites and Asters coming into a circle and holding on to each other. He only then realised that Sophie had healed all of the Affinites partially; enough for them to walk, but there were still obvious injuries. Reth, whose right leg had been broken in two places was walking with just a limp now, but his face looked as bloody and swollen as ever. Amisha Jasman, too, was walking just fine, but she was cradling a broken arm, while her daughter, Citra, was pressing a piece of ripped cloth against an obvious gash near her right temple.

As if in slow-motion, Matu saw Nathan run back from the door towards an open place in the circle. Nathan reached out and clasped his hands around Sky and Reth's arms. Right before the blue light of Sky's shimmer filled his vision, Matu saw the last of the roots snap, the wooden door break open, and a whole league of Disciples, double-bladed axes raised, stream into the prison hallway.

Blue light swept around them as they travelled from South America back to Saluverus in an instant. Matu prepared himself to let go of the Affinites the second they arrived in the Board Room, so that they could immediately shimmer off to Brazil and help their parents. They had to hurry. They had to make it in time...

When they shimmered into the Board Room, the room was more crowded than Matu had ever seen it before. Every member of the Small Council was there. All four Ceders were there, and so was Percy Kelly. They were all soaking wet and dripping water all over the floor. But then there were the three Elders as well, the oldest generation of Asters still living: Sky's grandfather, Sophie's grandmother, and Nathan's grandfather.

Matu beheld the scene. He stared at his father, but Diallo Madaki wouldn't meet his eyes. The three Elders stood to one side, their faces grim, and the Small Council stood near the corner desk, looking equally bleak. The round oak table had been moved to the side to make space for a large salt circle on the ground in the middle of the room. In the centre of the salt circle was a large, shallow dish filled with blood, and in the middle of the dish stood a thick candle. The candle wasn't lit anymore, but the thin wisp of smoke told Matu it had been not long ago.

"What's going on?" Sky demanded. Matu could feel his brother's anxiety mixed with anger rolling off him in waves.

Madeleine turned her face to the party that had just appeared. Her face was red and her eyes were blazing in anger. There was blood on her hands from a cut in her right palm. It was dripping to the floor. She must have been the one who had performed whatever spell had just been concluded. "Get them out, *now*," she spat.

It took Matu a moment to realise that she wasn't talking about the Asters, but the Affinites that they had saved. Abruptly, Sylvia Allen moved away from the rest of the Small Council and ushered the Affinites towards the Board Room's doors.

"To the Med Bay," Axel told Sylvia.

The Consul nodded to the Ambassador.

"I will go, too, and assist," Sophie's grandmother, Diana Griffiths, said solemnly. She walked to the door as well.

Josie squeezed Matu's hand and left with the other Affinites. Matu barely managed to tell her goodbye; his eyes were riveted on his father, who was staring at the ground. In all his life, Matu had never seen him look like this, so defeated.

The second the Board Room door closed, Sky shouted, "What the hell happened? They know Gayle's location; we need to go now!"

"Shut up!" Madeleine snapped at her son.

"We need to go!" Sky shouted back.

"Sky," Sophie said softly. She was staring at the salt circle on the ground, probably already knowing what all of it meant before any of the adults in the room explained.

"What?" Sky spat, turning to his sister.

"We got a call saying vitals were no longer being sent through from Cara and Tomas' chips," Rose Radbourne said. Her voice was calm, but there was something in her eyes that Matu had never seen before. Matu glanced at Nathan. He was looking at his mother with that clinical calmness that he always had during missions. The softness and kindness hadn't returned to him yet now that they were back. He was so unlike his mother in that respect; she remained kind and warm even out in the field.

All the Asters turned their heads to the screen behind them. While the images of the four Ceders present in the Board Room were still lit, the two images of Cara and Tomas Mendosa were dark. Which meant they were dead. No one needed to say the words because everyone already knew.

Before any of the Asters could ask the next question, Rose continued. "Madeleine did a tracking spell in Brazil. Gayle was alive then, but something was blocking her magic. We needed more power to break through the blockage to track her precise location and shimmer directly to her. With you all gone we brought in the Elders so we had two generations worth of magic, but once we cast the spell there was nothing. No hint of life or magic. Neither exists in this world anymore."

There was a deep sadness in Rose's voice. Her words struck each Aster to the core.

"The new King was smarter than we ever imagined," Rose continued. "He'd planned everything. Led us at every turn. His dark magic is potent. He matches Astaroth's power already at his young age. He cloaked everything; we didn't detect it already being in the town when we did our patrols."

"There was nothing we could have done," Katherine Griffiths finished.

Sky's mother was reeling in the corner. She was leaning on the chest of drawers, underneath the window and staring outside, the blood from her cut palm staining the wood. Her knuckles had turned white; that was how hard she was gripping the edge of the chest. In the awful silence that followed, no one moved.

"Say it," Sophie said through gritted teeth. She was staring at her mother, desperate to be wrong. "Someone needs to say it."

Katherine Griffiths straightened her back as she looked at her daughter. "Gayle Mendosa is gone. Her magic is gone."

Matu sucked in a breath.

Finally, Rose added the one thing that hit home for them all.

"The Queen is dead."

To be continued

Acknowledgements

Firstly, I want to thank my incredible dream team:

   Tina, for standing by me every step of the way from day one.

   Carlota, for always being there to be my sounding board.

   Timothy, for your everlasting energy and insights.

   Peggy, for your brilliant eye for detail.

Secondly, a thank you to my awe-inspiring parents. You are my heroes and I would have never made it this far without either of you.

Thirdly, let me thank my ridiculously talented designer, Arjuna Jay, who makes bringing my vision to life seem so easy. You can reach Arjuna at arjunajayofficial.artstation.com.

Finally, I am so grateful to a few more people who knew I would make it to this day:

   Nick, any time I veered off course, I remembered you telling me how at heart I was an author. Those words never failed to help me find my way back.

   Rob, every time you saw me you told me again of that empty space on your bookshelf where you would put my first novel. Now you can finally fill it.

   Juliette, you gave me such brilliant insights that improved my story-telling tremendously.

   Sanne, you helped to keep me believing in my stories and what they could become, as long as I didn't give up.

Marissa, you were there at the beginning. I don't think either of us thought that those original, silly ideas would ever turn into anything. But, oh my, look at what they have become.

From the author

Thank you for reading *A Queen To Come.* If you loved the book I would really appreciate it if you would take a moment to write a short review, as it will really help new readers find my books.

If you'd like to be kept informed about the progress of other books in the Aster series, free extra content, and more, visit my website francesellenbooks.com and sign up to my email list, or follow me on instagram.com/francesellen__/.

All the books in the Aster Prequel Novella series

A Queen To Come

A World To Lose

A Threat To Remain

A World To Lose

The second novella in the Asters Prequel Series.

The Queen has vanished from the face of the earth – her magic along with her. The impending threat that the Queen's birth predicted looms over the Asters as they now realise that they will one day have to face it without her.

But there is no time to grieve.

The Small Council still doesn't know what happened in Brazil that night, and they send Percy Kelly's best soldiers in to find out. But no soldier that goes in, ever comes back out.
Once again, they have fatally underestimated the unknown King of the South.

Meanwhile, the King of the North American Underworld is mobilising his troops. The rare magic he and his Disciples were so afraid of is no more, and he is taking his chance. The Asters are sent to the Grand Canyon to quell the uprising.

Despite their loss of faith in themselves, the Asters are still expected to protect the humans on the Surface of the world. They must pull together to stand any chance against the very first King they have ever faced.

FRANCES ELLEN
A WORLD TO LOSE
AN ASTER PREQUEL NOVELLA